The Wishing Hour

J. Adams

J. Adams

To Amanda,

my kindred spirit in the book world,

and the best nail tech to ever wield

a bottle of acrylic!

Take my heart into thy care,

and I shall leave a wish upon thine own,

that it lay open to me,

never hesitating to merge its beats with mine,

and in return,

my soul shall be thine for eternity.

S. G.

Zero

Venice, Italy

Standing on the steps of St. Mark's Basilica in the pouring rain, the warrior heaves a tired sigh and watches the battered creature from Lord Derth's army force its heavy body up and stand once again. The rain dilutes the sulfuric odor of the canal, lending a subtle freshness to the air. He inhales deeply, taking the cleansing scent into his lungs, carefully watching the creature.

The square is devoid of life, and if not for the storm, the only sound would be the gentle-flowing water of the canal. The fight has been brutal. It started at two am. It is now three. His sinewy muscles ache and his silky white shirt is streaked with blood, but his cuts have healed and his strength is quickly regenerating. Taking a calming breath, he pushes the long strands of inky black hair from his face. A leather thong holds the rest in place. His brilliant, blue cat-like eyes hold excellent night vision and clearly see the Urchin crouching, readying itself to spring once again. The creature's hands are like a hawk's talons and black leather stretches over the large round body. Its head is bald and pointed top teeth protrude over the bottom lip of the twisted and deformed mouth. Scars in different shapes and sizes cover the Urchin's face and neck, and the acidic green mucus dripping from its mouth is foul enough to turn the strongest of stomachs.

The warrior takes all of this in for a moment, then clears his mind. Closing his eyes, he calls upon the power living deep within him–a power summoned only when absolutely necessary. A rush of adrenaline fills his veins, heating his body to the core. Eyes snapping open, he lunges, meeting the Urchin in the air. He lands a fist in its chest, a great current of power surging from his hand as it makes contact with the Urchin's heart. As it cries out, the ear-piercing screech echoes throughout the square. No longer able to stand, it falls to the ground, writhing on the pavement.

He approaches the creature and stares down into its half-closed, blood-red eyes.

"This isn't over," it croaks in a gravelly voice.

"It is," he says, his voice conveying surety and strength. Standing as still as a statue of stone, the warrior watches the Urchin close its eyes and release a final rattly breath. It turns to dust and disintegrates before his eyes, the remains washed away by the rain. This is the second time this week he has witnessed such a sight, and he is sure it will not be the last.

Heaving a deep sigh, his gaze moves to the body lying a few yards behind him. Scooping the unconscious woman up in his arms, he cradles her against him. Once again he has succeeded in protecting her, only this time it had been a closer call than before. His eyes take in the soaked features of the woman he has come to know as his true mate. Every time he touches her, the mark of the *Ki Talimai*, the soul's bond, glows and tingles in his palm. Now, as he stands holding her in his arms, the eternal mark burns.

Lowering his dark head, the warrior presses his forehead against hers, inhaling her rain-enhanced scent, a mixture of jasmine, vanilla and cinnamon pine on her skin. He knows her scent well because it matches his own. It calls out to him as strongly as her senses. He knows her emotions intimately–her joys, her fears, her sorrows, her grief, her loneliness. He knows *her*. Yet she doesn't know the real him, nor the full measure of his powers.

But she will. She will finally know everything this night.

* * *

As he moves toward the large double doors of the church, they swing open without him making contact. He never needs to touch an object to move it, he simply thinks it into action and his command is obeyed. When it comes to people or living creatures, however, his powers only work on the weak-minded. For the strong, he must get physical. Even still, he never forces his will on anyone. He would never abuse his powers that way. That had been the first lesson he was taught when his training began seven hundred years ago at the young age of twenty.

Ducking his head, he steps inside and Father Battiano silently directs him to the corridor to the right. He has been here before and had used the same quarters he now enters. He silently lets his eyes scan the room. There is a small bed against the wall, covered with a thick quilt. A pan of water is heating on a hotplate in the corner and a creaky furnace warms the small area. A wooden door in the corner opens to a small bathroom.

Walking past the priest, the warrior places the woman on the bed, then asks him to turn and face the wall.

When the holy man complies, he in turn closes his eyes and whispers three words. In an instant, the woman is dry and now wearing a soft white gown. Lifting her from the bed, he pulls the quilt and top sheet back, gently tucking her underneath. Taking a moment to study her, his eyes move over her smooth brown skin, long fluttering lashes, and mass of black spiraled curls splaying over the white pillow, spilling down to her waist. He watches the slow rise and fall of her chest, listening to her soft rhythmic breathing. Then his gaze moves back to her face, and like thousands of other times, he admires her beauty. From the moment she was born, he has been watching over her from afar until recently. He witnessed her childhood, watched her blossom and grow and turn into the great beauty that she is.

Lifting her hand to his lips, he presses his palm against hers and her *Ki Talimai* calls to his, causing heat to spread up his arm through his entire body. Never before has it affected him so strongly. And he knows why.

Her call to him is stronger because the bond between them is near to completion. When that happens, nothing in this world or any other can ever come between them. They will fully lay claim on one another's hearts, and souls.

This is not their end.

It is only the beginning.

One

The dimly-lit room is cold, but I am warm. The creak of the water heater and the beating of rain against the stone walls is soothing, as well as the faint musky scent of the old building and the softness of freshly-washed sheets. Though my eyes are still closed, I am awake enough to sense a familiar presence surrounding me–a presence that defies all description. *His* essence pierces my very soul, sustains me, and it has for a week now. He is my protector, my conscience, my guide, my archangel.

Yet I still don't know his name.

The arms holding me now are as familiar to me as my own name. And the steady heartbeat encased in the rock-solid, muscular chest my head is resting upon fills me with complete peace. After what I've been through, I need that peace. Slowly opening my eyes, I turn slightly, raising my gaze to the piercing blue of his and my heartbeat speeds up. I smile, the reality of his nearness threatening to overwhelm me. When he smiles back, the rest of the room fades away. At this moment, the fear I have carried with me is forgotten.

"Are you well?" he asks in that familiar, deep voice of his.

"Yes."

He continues to stare intently and I want to say more, anything more, but no words come. I can't lend voice to my thoughts. So I silently wait to hear his angelic voice again. It is the sweetest sound in existence, and nothing is more beautiful to my ears. He touches my face, trailing a warm finger down my cheek.

"There is much to say."

This is true, for I feel his emotions travel through me before his words give voice to his thoughts. I should be used to it by now, but each time he looks into my eyes, each time he touches me, the sensation is renewed, and my senses are freshly captured by his.

Helping me sit up, he keeps his arms around me, holding me close. Their shelter is one I never want to leave because his warmth is so intoxicating. The haven of his embrace feels like home.

"Do you remember the very moment we met?" he asks.

"Of course." I burrow deeper in his embrace. The moment I met him is one I will never forget.

* * *

One week ago.

Grandville, Colorado

Sitting in the living room of my small apartment, I absently stare out the window into the wooded area behind my building, once again allowing my thoughts to run rampant. These times of aimlessness are coming more frequently because I have absolutely no life. This discovery is nothing new, but for some reason, today that fact is more prominent. When I tell people I have no life, they usually laugh and say something like, "Yeah, right," or "You're joking, right?" I've never been able to understand why they don't believe me.

Glimpsing my reflection in the window, I attempt to smile without success. I am twenty-five years old, six feet tall, black, and single. And except for Henry, my husky Persian cat, I live a solitary life. Always have. There are no siblings, no cousins, no aunts, uncles, or grandparents. Having lost my mother to cancer three years before and my father to heart disease the year after that, I have been flying solo for a while now. And thanks to the insurance money I received from my parents' death, as well as some wise investing, I only work a couple of days a week at a rest home, helping to care for the elderly residents there. Every now and then–even when I am not scheduled to work–I go in for a few hours and help out. I've really grown to love the people I tend to. There is definitely a wealth of forgotten wisdom in that place and I enjoy hearing the thoughts of the loving old souls residing there.

So believe it or not, this is the extent of my social life.

It's Friday night, and once again there is yelling next door. Karen's husband has been drinking again and is on a warpath. Though I have become used to the sound, tonight things are different. Karen is screaming even louder, her little girl's sorrowful cries echoing throughout our floor of the apartment building. The sound makes my heart ache. She is only five and is forced to witness things no child should ever have to see. There have been so many times over the past couple of months that I've encouraged Karen to take her daughter and leave. I've tried to help her understand things will only get worse. But she never listens. She says she loves him too much.

Listening to her pleas, it really has gotten worse.

I pick up the phone to call the police when there is a soft knock at my door. Hesitantly, I approach the door until I hear the small voice of Karen's daughter Sarah whispering, "Celine, can I come in?"

Throwing caution the wind, I quickly open the door and pull her inside, locking all three locks behind me. I pick up her small frame and she clings to me as I return to the chair in front of the window. I call the police and they inform me that they are sending an officer out. Waiting, I stare out into the woods and hold Sarah close, softly humming, trying to mute the screams of her mother. Listening to the painfully frightening sound, I press my chin in the little girl's hair as tears fill my eyes, blurring my vision. When they fall onto my face and my vision clears, I glimpse something that causes my mouth to drop open.

A most astounding being appears amidst the trees.

I must be seeing things. Closing my eyes, I rub hard before opening them again. He is still there.

His straight, jet-black, hair hangs around his shoulders and his tanned, lean-muscled physique is clad in a white, form-fitting silk shirt tucked into black leather leggings and high black boots. He has to be at least seven feet tall! Even from where I sit, high up in the window, he looks magnificent, the most glorious looking man I have ever seen. He makes the models on the front of romance novels look like pansies.

As he walks forward, his eyes are clearly focused on me and my cheeks warm. He stops and raises a hand, his smile wide. Completely shocked and awed that this amazing being is smiling at *me,* I lift my hand in return, startled by a sudden loud banging on my door. I jump up and Sarah whimpers.

"Give me my kid, Celine!" Roger's voice is slurred but deceiving. He may be drunk, but he is huge, and still as strong as an ox.

Holding Sarah close, I frantically wonder where the police are. When my eyes move back to the woods, the man is no longer there. Disengaging myself from Sarah long enough to grab my purse, I dump out the contents to find my can of pepper spray, but before I can pick it up where it has fallen to the floor, the door is kicked open and we both scream. Backing against the wall, I cling to Sarah, not knowing what to do.

Roger snarls like a crazed animal and lunges toward us. Picking up a large metal paperweight, I prepare to throw it at him, hoping my aim is true, but it is unnecessary. He has only taken two steps when a force flies through the door, slamming him to the floor. I hear the crack of Roger's nose as it hits the hard tile. Shocked, I finally look up at our rescuer.

It is him! The man from the woods!

From a distance he had been magnificent, but up close, he is indescribably magnanimous! His head almost brushes the ceiling and he's even taller than I thought, at least eight feet! He's a giant! His cat-like blue gaze pierces me to the core. Reaching out a strong hand, he gently places it on my shoulder and I almost forget to breathe.

"Are you all right, Celine?" he asks. His deep angelic voice is heavily accented. He sounds Italian, but it's more like a mixture of European accents.

"Yes," I breathe, staring up at him. "But . . . how did you know? And how do you know my name?"

He smiles and answers simply, "I just know."

I swallow hard, not knowing what to say. For the first time in my life, I am completely speechless.

Sarah turns in my arms, looking up at the man curiously. He squats his long, sinewy body down in front of her, taking her small hand in his large one.

"Everything will be all right, Sarah. You and your mother will never be hurt by him again." He presses a hand to her cheek. "You believe me, don't you?"

She nods, returning his smile. Seeming satisfied, he stands, turning his beautiful face to me, and stares silently for a long moment. Feeling like I am melting before him, I lean against the desk for support, fearing I will fall right at his feet.

"Who are you?" I finally manage to ask.

Instead of answering, he reaches out and takes my hand, entwining my fingers with his. His hands are huge! My breath catches and I tighten my hold. Knowing nothing about this man, I am comfortable sharing this intimate gesture with him. Something inside me is drawn to him, whispering to my soul that I am completely safe with him. And suddenly it doesn't matter who he is. My heart knows him and that is all that matters.

"Do you trust me?" he asks.

"Yes," I answer without hesitation.

"Then trust me when I tell you we are connected in ways I cannot explain right now." He pauses, squeezing my hand, causing warmth to rush over me. "One day I will explain, but for now, please know I speak the truth."

I *do* trust him. I have no idea why, and it's unbelievable that I can feel this way about someone I have never met until today. But everything inside me knows him and what I feel for him runs deep. Call me crazy, but this is how I feel. And indeed, most would think I *am* crazy. Heck, if I were to allow myself to think about it too much, I would believe it too! So I don't.

"I trust you," I say with surety, pressing my palm against his. "I trust you."

* * *

There are sirens blaring in the distance.

"Finally," I mumble.

"Celine," he says softly, "we must leave. Get your purse and come with me."

"But what about Sarah? I can't just leave her like this."

"She and her mother will be fine." His eyes move to the unconscious man on the floor.

"But . . ."

"Celine, you said you trusted me."

I pause, looking up into his eyes. "I do." Saying nothing more, I put everything back in my purse, grab Henry, and then we take Sarah and my cat next door.

When we enter, Karen is sitting on the sofa holding her head in her hands, crying softly.

"Mommy!"

At the sound of her daughter's voice, she looks up and opens her arms. Sarah runs into them and Karen presses her battered face into the little girl's hair.

As my protector walks over and quickly kneels before mother and child, Karen's eyes widen in surprise and awe, and I can definitely understand. The word magnificent again comes to mind as I watch him.

"Depending on your choice, all will be well now." His voice is firm but kind. "You and your daughter will be safe, but only if you take the initiative now to make it so."

She nods, understanding him perfectly, and I can't help but wonder why she never listened to me when I advised her to do the same thing. In any case, I'm glad she is listening now.

We hear the sirens outside the apartment building and he stands, taking my hand.

"We must go now," he says.

I nod and give Sarah my cat. "Take care of him for me."

"But where are you . . ."

We leave before I can hear the rest of Karen's question, but I finish it in my head, knowing I wouldn't have had an answer for her anyway.

He leads me from Karen's apartment back to my own. Guiding me to the window, he opens it and takes out the screen. Lifting me in his arms, he whispers, "Put your arms around me and hold on tight."

Nodding, I close my eyes, pressing my face against his neck. My heart is pounding, but I know he will let no harm come to me. Keeping my eyes closed, I feel the breeze rush over us as he jumps from the third story window, landing so softly on his feet, I barely realize we are on the ground.

We travel through the woods at an incredible speed–too fast for me to try and focus. So I keep my face pressed against his neck, soaking in the warmth of his body and the scent of his skin. Both are completely intoxicating. I have no idea where we are going and no words are spoken between us, but then again, no words are needed. Every so often, his embrace tightens and he pulls me further into himself, as if he is sheltering me from any and all harm.

My thoughts travel to Sarah and Karen, and I hope she will indeed take my protector's advice and press charges against Roger to keep her daughter safe. I wish I had been able to say a more proper goodbye and grab a few of my clothes and personal items, but there hadn't been time. I suppose I can pick up a few things somewhere, and at least I have my checkbook and debit card. Now, if only I knew our destination.

Two

Minutes later, we stop beside a secluded little stream. Completely stiff as he puts me down, I take a moment to stretch and allow my stomach to catch up to the rest of my body. My hair is wind-blown, my lips slightly chapped, and I feel like my head has been stuck outside the window of a speeding car. Moistening my lips, I run my fingers back through my hair, knowing I must look a sight.

He smiles and deep dimples appear, making him even more handsome. "I will be right back."

"Wait. Where are you going?" The sky is beginning to darken and I am frightened of being left in the woods alone, especially since I have no idea where we are or if we are even in Colorado anymore.

He squeezes my hand. "I am not going far. I promise."

"Okay." Releasing his hand, I draw some courage to the surface and sit on a large boulder, watching him disappear through the trees. My eyes scan the darkening forest for wildlife and I nervously listen for the pitter-patter of forest creatures, praying I won't be eaten by a mountain lion. The temperature has dropped a few degrees and fall is heavy in the air. Shivering a little, I rub the goose bumps on my arms.

Shaking my head, I wonder how I allowed myself to be lured away from my home and my life. I have no idea where we are going or what we are even doing. My life up to this point has been pretty boring, but the decisions I've made today have been crazy–no, they've been beyond crazy. And I *never* do crazy! I've never been one to take chances or act spontaneously, and I've never ventured out of my comfort zone, or *any* zone. But there is a first time for everything.

I have only been lost in analytical thought for less than a minute when he appears, holding two overnight travel bags wrapped in clear plastic. One is red, the other, navy blue. He hands me the red one.

"We must change and be on our way. There is a private plane waiting for us."

"What? What do you mean? Where are we–"

"I will answer your questions once we are on the plane and safely on our way."

My mind is a whirlwind of questions, but for the moment, I mentally push them back and open the case, finding a couple of neatly-folded outfits. Pulling out a pair of black slacks, a peach shell and cardigan, and a black leather blazer, I wonder how he knew my size, and then I remind myself that he knows *me*. And as strange as this fact is, I know *him*.

Draping the clothes over my arm, I turn, freezing at the sight of him pulling off his white shirt, taking another from the bag. My mouth falling open slightly, I take in his smooth, chiseled physique. He has the body of a giant Greek statue, every sinewy muscle carved to perfection. When he catches me staring and smiles, I clear my throat and turn away. Modesty makes me want to go into the trees to change, but I am afraid of losing sight of him.

Seeming to read my thoughts, he turns his back to me saying, "I promise not to look. Your privacy is your own."

Trusting his word completely, I quickly strip and change, tucking my dirty clothes into the bag.

"Thank you," I say and he turns back to me, smiling as his eyes travel over me. Again, my cheeks warm.

"You are very welcome."

Using the brush and mirror in the bag, I make my hair a little more presentable. There is a black hair scrunchie in the bag as well and I use it to pull my hair back in a ponytail, but as usual, a few tendrils escape and fall against my face no matter how hard I try to keep them in place.

Zipping the bag, I ask, "How are we getting to the airport? We can't keep traveling like this or I'll need to change again."

"We are not going to the airport. A friends owns a plane and has an airstrip on his property. As for getting there . . ." Leaving his answer unfinished, he dashes through the trees, returning seconds later pushing a large motorcycle. "The main road is only a few minutes away." He straps the two bags on the back.

I take a deep breath. "You've thought of everything."

"It was important that I did." His deep voice is fervent.

"Why?" The questions have moved to the forefront of my mind again. "Why am I here with you? Why did you come to me? And who *are* you?"

"I am here to protect you. For now, I can tell you no more than that." Taking my hand, he presses his large palm against mine and it produces a tingling sensation. When I start to pull my hand away, he tightens his grip gently, looking at me intently. "Your life has a greater purpose than you know. I am here to help you fulfill that purpose and protect you from those who would see you fail." Just as my mind begins its tumble into a mass of confusion, he moves closer, pressing his lips against my ear and softly says, "I am here for you, Celine. You are the very reason I exist."

I don't realize I've stopped breathing until my head is resting against his chest. I release a shaky breath.

Plain old boring me? Me, Celine Anderson, here for a special purpose? Well then, that changes things.

I have no idea what lies before me, but every dull day I have lived so far is worth this one shared day with him. There has never been anyone special in my life and I have never been in anything remotely resembling a relationship. Now I understand why. And though I still have questions, for now, I let them wait.

When he finally releases my hand, I turn it over and suck in a breath. In the middle of my palm there is a mark shaped like two rings connected together. It almost looks like a light brand. I hold my hand up for him to see.

"What is this?"

He hesitates a moment before answering. "It is a *Ki Talimai*, the mark of the soul's bond."

"Soul's bond?" Of course, I am even more confused. "What is a soul's bond? And how did I get it?"

"In my world the soul's bond is the strongest and most powerful of bonds."

"Your world? What do you mean? Where did you come from?"

"I wish I could tell you right now, but I can't. Please believe me. It is in your best interest, as well as others, that I keep that information to myself."

He is again hesitant, awaiting my response. I know he truly does want to tell me, and he desperately needs me to believe what he is telling me now. I can feel it without him saying the words.

"Can you tell me anything at all?" I ask, holding the branded hand out to him.

He smiles warmly, taking it in his. "Once we are on the plane I will share what I can." He squeezes my hand. "We must go."

"All right." I ask nothing more, trusting he will keep his word.

He puts on a leather jacket and we walk the motorcycle up to the main road. When we reach it, he hands me a helmet.

"I have never been on a motorcycle before," I tell him as I put the helmet on and fasten the strap. Filled with nervous excitement, I wonder how I can be this nervous about riding a motorcycle when we traveled even faster as he carried me across the miles on foot. I chalk my erratic thinking up to this new experience of trusting someone with my life so completely.

Putting his own helmet on (most likely for my benefit) and hopping on in front of me, he turns slightly. "Do not be nervous. I will keep you safe."

"I know," I say, wrapping my arms around his waist as he starts the ignition. I chuckle inwardly, musing that I feel a little like a daring teenager running off with a handsome bad boy. A *very* handsome bad boy.

Sighing, I press myself against his warm back as we head down the lone stretch of road through the darkness.

Three

As we speed through the black night, my arms are tightly wrapped around his waist, my cheek pressed against his back. Closing my eyes, I again wonder how all of this has happened. Just this morning I pondered what I was going to do with the rest of my life. It had been stagnant, boring, and lonely, and I was mentally preparing to be a frequent flier at the rest home until I wound up there, myself.

But that was this morning. Without thought, I left everything behind and am now riding on the back of a motorcycle, holding on to this wonderful man–no, he is more than a man. Sighing, I breathe in his intoxicating scent as it fans my face in the wind–a deliciously sensuous smell that brings to mind the freshness of fall and warm winter holidays, and it is totally wreaking havoc on my senses. I take a deep breath, trying to slow my heartbeat, because the last thing I want is to pass out and fall off the motorcycle. That would not be good at all. I could try to analyze why he is having such a powerful effect on me, but I choose not to. The *why* does not matter.

There are no street lights and the canyon road is shrouded in darkness. With the absence of traffic I can see nothing, yet I am not anxious at all. In fact, I feel an unnatural sense of calm–well, unnatural for me, anyway. The even sound of the motorcycle's engine fills my ears and I imagine it has taken on a rhythm, a beat that plays only for us. Glancing up, I take in the stars shining faintly in the overcast sky. Some people can tell the direction they are going just by gazing up at the stars. However, I am *not* one of those people. If I were lost and alone, the stars would do me no good because I am directionally challenged. I would probably just stay lost, only to be found in the woods a week later in a condition that would definitely earn me a long stay in a room with padded walls and no door knob.

Absently, I tighten my arms around him. A second later I feel one of his hands press against one of mine and squeeze gently, reassuring me. My face warms, making me grateful for the cool wind on my cheeks.

After another few minutes, there are lights glowing from various homes in the mountainside, like beacons being lit to reassure us that we are on the right path. Finally exiting the mountains, we ride out into flat lands devoid of trees. Approaching a paved private drive, he turns onto it. The drive stretches for about a mile and at the end sits a massive log cabin that looks more like a mansion. Half the windows are lit and the outer lights are on, giving the home a wondrous look of enchantment. He parks the motorcycle in the circular driveway and shuts the engine off. Helping me off, he grabs our bags.

"Come," he says softly, taking my hand. Saying nothing, I simply follow, realizing now that I'm going to be doing a lot of that.

Before we can even reach the door, it opens, and once again, my mouth drops open and I am rendered speechless. The man standing in the tall doorway could be my protector's brother, the only difference being skin and hair coloring. While my escort's hair is an inky black, which stands out against his tan skin yet suits his handsome features perfectly, the other man owns a mane of spun gold atop pale skin. Their chiseled features and height are about the same. The mold must have been broken after they made these two because surely there can't be more of them. But then what do I know? At this point, not much–only that I have put my life in the hands of a beautiful man who still has not told me his name. This *so* goes against my normal grain. And though I am still concerned, I am not afraid. It is as if everything inside me knows I can trust him, which means I pretty much trust his friend, too.

"Is everything ready?" my protector asks the blond.

"Yes." His eyes move to me and he smiles, opening the door wider, allowing us to enter. He has a lovely smile, a comforting one that tells me somehow everything is going to be fine.

I immediately begin to scan my surroundings, never in my life having been in a home so grand. I look up at the massive crystal chandelier, then down at the gray marbled tile flooring. The entryway is surrounded by cherry wood molding and the place even smells elegant. There is a spiraled wooden staircase leading up to the second and third floor. How I would love to go exploring, but obviously now is not the time to indulge such a fantasy.

As we follow the blond down a long art-lined hallway, I gawk at the large gold-framed paintings on the walls. I am no art critic, but they sure look expensive to me. I would bet my right arm they are originals. Nothing in this house seems to be done halfway and everything looks like big ticket items.

Turning left, we enter a very roomy, immaculate kitchen that would be a professional chef's dream. Then we follow him through the kitchen to a set of French doors leading out the back of the house. During all this time, nothing has been said, not a word spoken, as if speaking is a waste of time. I wish someone would say something, because my thoughts are running a mile a minute.

Across the large lawn sits a jet on an airstrip. The engine is running and a female attendant is standing at the bottom of the steps, I assume waiting for us. As we stop on the patio, the men turn to each other and the blond hands my protector a large yellow envelope.

"This is everything. When you arrive, a car will be waiting. The house is secluded and well stocked. You should have everything you need."

He places a hand on the blond's shoulder. "*Grazie,* my friend, for everything."

"You are welcome, my brother. And may the blessings of *The One* go with you." He turns to me, bowing deeply and I smile.

My protector unzips the front pocket of his travel bag and places the envelope inside, then turns to me, taking my hand. "Let us go, *cara mia.*"

Quickly making our way across the green lawn, we return the attendant's welcome and board the plane. I'm so tired I practically drop into one of the soft leather seats. After removing the envelope from the bag, he sits in the seat directly across from me, giving us the perfect view of one another. Now that we are on the plane, my first instinct is to demand that he tell me where we are going, but I bite my tongue. I know he will keep his word, and no matter where it is, he will keep me safe.

He smiles at me, as if he is reading my mind and says, "We are going to Italy."

"Italy? As in Venice, Rome, and Florence Italy?"

"As in Venice, Rome, and Florence," he answers, laughing. "Only just Venice."

The sound of his deep laugh takes me off guard, it is so alluring, just like everything else about him.

As the plane begins down the runway, I grab the arm of my seat. I have only flown once in my life and that flight was only a couple of hours long, but this time it will be hours and hours. I try not to let my nervousness show on my face. Evidently I'm not doing too good a job because he quickly unbuckles his seat belt and switches seats, sitting in the one next to me. Taking my hand, he stretches his long legs out in front of him.

"Everything will be fine," he says to me and I immediately feel calmer. I squeeze his hand, receiving a warm smile in return.

As soon as we are in the air, I look out the window, but darkness veils the expansive sky, making me feel very small in the universe.

Glancing at the large yellow envelope on his lap, curiosity again burns my insides. "You promised to tell me what you could."

"And I will." He opens his mouth to say more when some mild turbulence causes me to grip his hand tighter, practically cutting off his circulation, though he doesn't complain. "Everything is fine," he repeats softly. "We are safe."

Meeting his gaze is momentarily like glimpsing the sun. His face is exquisite, and that I am with him defies all reason. There has to have been some sort of mistake. It isn't really me he is here for.

"There is no mistake," he says, reading my mind.

"Stop that," I say, feeling completely exposed, realizing now that my every thought is being picked up by him.

"I cannot help it. Your emotions call to me and I must answer."

I *am* exposed.

"Your emotions affect me deeply, *cara*."

Taking a deep breath to clear my head, I struggle to control my thoughts. The questions can no longer wait. "Why are we going to Venice?"

Holding my hand between his, he looks at me intently. "Because it is a place I know well. I was born there, in the year 1290."

I laugh, sure that he is kidding. When his expression doesn't change, I sober a bit. "But . . . how can that be? That would make you . . ." Pausing, I do the math in my head. "That would make you seven hundred and twenty years old. How is that possible?"

"That is something I cannot explain at the moment. But trust that I am telling you the truth."

That goes without saying. As unbelievable as what he's telling me may seem, deep inside I know he would not lie to me. Maybe I am mentally connected to his thoughts as well.

"You are," he says.

"How can this be?" I breathe.

"How does not matter. Just know that we are connected in a way most people could never dream of."

I take a moment to let his comment settle. "But I don't even know your name. Are you going to tell me?"

"Once a man gives his name, he gives power over himself. Those of my kind are taught this when we are young." He squeezes my hand. "I cannot tell you now because it would put you in even more danger, but I will soon." He holds my eyes with his. "Can you trust this for now?"

I am disappointed and he knows this, but I nod. Trying to stifle a yawn, a wave of fatigue comes over me and I am suddenly too tired for more questions. He pushes a button on a panel above us.

"Yes?" the flight attendant's voice answers through the speaker.

"We need a blanket and a pillow, please."

"Right away, sir." A minute later she appears with his request.

"Is Italy as beautiful as they say?" I ask sleepily.

"It is very beautiful. But while Rome, Tuscany and Florence have green rolling hills, Venice has a beauty all it's own. You will see."

Nodding, I yawn again.

"You are tired, Celine. You should rest."

I want to disagree, but I really do need to sleep. Too much excitement for one day. I recline my seat back and he tucks the pillow behind my head, and then covers me with the blanket. As he leans over me, I gaze up into his piercing eyes. His face is that of an angel, and I will never tire of looking at him.

He presses his hand against my cheek. "Rest, *cara*," he whispers as his soft lips touch my brow.

Closing my eyes, I hear nothing else.

* * *

Leaning back in his seat, the warrior silently watches her drift into a peaceful slumber. Taking in her fluttering eyelids, he watches the slow rise and fall of her chest. He leans in closer, feeling the soft exhale of her breath on his face. It is a most sweet sensation. How he loves just looking at her! He could spend forever just gazing at her, and he wishes this moment could last, that she could always be safe. If he could shelter her from what will undoubtedly come, he would.

The Urchin had been very close to finding her. He could feel it in his bones and knew it had been time to take her into hiding. He could take no chances, because she is too important and her survival is vital.

Watching the pulse beat at the base of her neck, he finds the beat of his own heart is keeping in time with hers. In all the many years of his life, he has never felt for anyone the smallest measure of what he does for her. He never could, because his heart had been hers all along.

When he began his training, he had already known he would have a part in the prophecy, and now, having come to know with absolute certainty the full extent of what his part will be, he experiences renewed awe and is again overwhelmed.

He will see this through, for it is no longer just his duty to protect Celine. It is his destiny.

She is his destiny.

Four

Jolted awake by the sound of the plane's wheels touching down on the runway, I open my eyes, squinting against the sunlight shining through the window, unable to believe I slept through the whole trip. Turning, I find him watching me and I wonder if he has slept at all, or if he even needs sleep.

"Yes, I do," is his reply to my unvoiced question. "I just don't need as much sleep as the average human."

"There is definitely nothing average about you," I say, giving him a tired smile.

His hand covers mine. "Nothing at all." He opens the yellow envelope and takes out a passport. "This is for you."

Opening it, I glance at my photo a moment before flipping through it. It is even stamped already. There is no point in me asking how he managed it, so I don't.

He gestures out the window. "This is a privately owned airstrip. We are half an hour away from Venice."

I look out the opposite window. The whole area is paved and there are a few small planes parked a short distance away. And they *all* look expensive. It seems all his connections are very affluent. Looking out the other window again, I peer at the small white building with a control tower on top.

"Since there are no cars in Venice, we will take the train into St. Marks Square then take a water bus from there."

I've seen photos of Venice in travel magazines and read that the through streets are canals, but that is *all* I know. Despite not knowing what I am heading into, I am excited and eagerly anticipating seeing the city, myself.

When we get off the plane, a black Mercedes sedan is waiting to take us to the train station. The driver's face is expressionless as he opens the door for us. He and my protector nod at each other before we get in, and we are immediately on our way.

* * *

No words my brain can come up with will ever do justice to the sight before me. Venice is incredible! Coming out of the train station and entering St. Mark's square, my eyes dart everywhere at once as I try to take everything in.

The huge, old buildings are various colors of stucco and old brick, and the palaces along the canal boast elegant arched windows, some with colorful flower boxes lining them. Shops line the walkways, heavy with the traffic of tourists as they bustle in and out of doorways carrying bags of souvenirs.

But the crowing glory of the square is St. Mark's Basilica, the most famous church in Venice. The granite and stone building is a glorious work of art, covered in arches and topped with dozens of steeples. I stop and stare in wonder.

Feeling the warm squeeze of my hand, I turn my awe-filled gaze to my protector, and the feeling inside me is magnified as his adamant gaze produces in me the same wonder.

Gripping the straps of both our bags in one hand, he keeps his other firmly wrapped around mine as we walk down to the docks to hire a water bus, attracting a few stares from tourists along the way, which cannot be helped. It isn't everyday that you see a gorgeous eight-foot god walking by.

When we reach the dock, there is a boat already waiting. Evidently he knows the driver because when we are seated, the man heads out, obviously already knowing where to take us.

We ride in silence, his hand holding mine, the hum of the boat engine filling our ears, and I relish the breeze whipping through my hair as I take in the passing scenery. Since it is still tourist season, the walkways are packed and I am glad we don't have to walk the distance and shovel through hoards of people.

After another moment, we exit the canal and head out to a small island in the distance.

"It is called the Lidoro," he tells me. "The island is completely private. There is a boat there as well, so we won't need the water bus to get back and forth. Not that we would anyway."

"A whole island to ourselves?" I am incredulous.

"It is necessary."

I raise a furrowed brow. "Am I really in that much danger?"

Turning his blue gaze to mine, he softly answers, "You are, *cara.*"

Nodding, I swallow hard against the nervousness rising inside me. Until now, I've somehow remained calm, and it is only now that I truly begin to understand how real this all is. And I *still* don't *fully* understand.

"I know you don't understand," he says. "But you will– soon."

Looking into his eyes, I again choose to trust him and let it go.

When we reach the dock, the driver helps me off the boat. My protector grabs our bags and turns to the man. "Are all the precautions in place?"

"*Si*. Everything is taken care of. No one will get near the island."

"*Grazie*."

As the driver steers away, my protector takes my hand and we begin our walk up the wide cobbled path through a large grove of trees. The trees form a tunnel, curving over the path meeting each other, and sunlight softly filters through the leafy limbs. Lifting my gaze upward, I feel its warmth on my face.

"This is so beautiful," I whisper.

"It is. And it only gets better."

As we exit the trees, I see how true his words are.

The villa is breathtaking. The outside is beige stucco and brick. The top of each window is rounded, the bottom of several of them lined with flower boxes. A granite fountain sits in the middle of the wide circular walkway. The wooden door is a deep mahogany with a black iron ring attached.

"Wow!" is all I manage to get out and he smiles, then pulls a key from his pocket, unlocking the door.

The elegant entryway, tiled in tan, is lit by a massive iron and crystal chandelier. He gives me a tour of the house, his height forcing him to duck through each doorway. The furnishings are a mix of antique, upholstered, and modern Italian leather pieces. The decor is also a combination of modern and baroque. Everything is spotless and the house smells of cinnamon apple. The kitchen is completely updated with metallic graphite appliances, including a large subzero refrigerator. The fridge and the cupboards are completely stocked. Beneath the kitchen floor is a cellar that holds a year's food supply. Taking all of this in, I imagine a team of people combing the house, getting everything in order for our arrival.

He takes my hand, leading me upstairs. There are five bedrooms and four bathrooms on the middle floor and another five bedrooms and three bathrooms on the third floor. Each is elegant and uniquely designed. Walking back down to the second floor, he turns to me, lacing his long fingers through mine.

"I would tell you to pick any room you would like, but I prefer having you closer to me, so I have chosen the room across the hall from mine for you. The middle floor is also the most convenient for me."

I am both comforted and disturbed, if a person can really feel both at the same time. I will feel more secure being so close to him, but the other feelings I carry inside will most likely make it next to impossible to sleep with him right across the hall.

"This will be fine," I say, quickly pushing the thoughts from my mind. With his telepathic abilities enabling him to read my thoughts so easily, I will have to be more careful in controlling them. Allowing my gaze to travel around the room, I take everything in. In the middle of the room sits a high, queen-size bed covered in rich beige and green linens. A flat screen television is mounted to the wall over a cozy fireplace and a brown leather couch with corded pillows sits in front of it. It is absolutely beautiful.

"You will find everything you need in the dresser and closet."

Walking over to the ivory dresser, I open the top drawer, then another and another. All are completely filled with clothes. Everything still has tags attached and is exactly my size. I can't believe it.

"How did you do all this?" I ask, completely astonished.

"I have had a long time to plan."

Silently pondering his words, I walk through the spacious bathroom, stopping for a moment in front of the ivory marbled vanity, taking in the treasures atop it. An exquisite wooden comb and brush set sits on a mirrored silver tray along with a silver box containing a variety of hair accessories. A basket of new cosmetics is to the right of the tray. I stare in renewed wonder another moment before entering the walk-in closet, gasping softly. The whole back wall is lined with clothes and the shelves are filled with designer shoes and handbags, all Italian made.

"Well, I guess I won't need to shop after all."

"I know you want to tour the city, but for now, it is imperative that you remain on the island, for your own protection. I need to keep you as safe as possible."

I heave a disappointed sigh, resigned to staying put. I figured if I had to be in Venice, at least I could do some sightseeing, but I was mistaken.

"There are many sights to see right here on the island," he says, taking my hand, the warmth of his voice seeping into my emotions, soothing me. "I promise you will not be bored."

Looking into his eyes, I smile. "I could never be bored with you." With the squeeze of his hand, I know he believes me, and somehow, everything will be okay.

* * *

Three days later.

On the mainland in a dark alleyway, the Urchin stands over the boatman's lifeless body. It had followed the man three days ago, watching as he took the two passengers out to the secluded island. Then it waited for his return, planning to corner him alone somewhere.

The Urchin-kind must not be seen by humans. This is the law of the Underground, the Urchin's home. They are not allowed to be seen because the knowledge of their existence would hinder their leader's goal of stopping the prophecy from coming to pass. The Urchin-kind exist for one reason and one reason only: to fulfill this mission. They will see the mission through and be successful, even if their lives are lost in the process. Lord Derth, their leader, would have it no other way.

Hearing a light noise, the Urchin crouches, scanning its surroundings for a moment. Locating the source of the sound, a small food wrapper being blown to and fro by the wind, it relaxes again. The creature hadn't been able to catch the man alone that first night, so it waited for another opportunity to arise. Tonight it had. The Urchin had spotted the boatman exiting a bar, staggering as he made his way down the dark alley, and right into its hands. It had been so easy to take his life. A quick snap of the neck and the man was no more.

Humans are fragile weaklings, it thinks as it lowers itself to the man's body. With the closing of its claws, a sharp blade emerges from a small hole between the joints with a tube attached. Most of its kind dislike this procedure because it causes a great deal of pain, but the creature isn't like the others. It has done this so many times, the pain is almost non-existent.

The creature sticks the blade in the man's neck and extracts some blood through the tube. Then it stands and waits for the blood to take effect. After a couple of moments, the deed is complete.

Five

Smiling across the table at my protector, we begin eating dinner. Thanks to the shelf of Italian cookbooks in the pantry and the amazing kitchen I've been able to work in, I do pretty well at cooking some of the native dishes. Tonight we are dining on field greens salad, chicken marsala with garlic potatoes, and sauteed mixed vegetables. For dessert there is raspberry *gelato*. Since neither of us drink, we sip chilled sparkling grape juice.

The past three days have been full of wonder and more enjoyable than I imagined they could be. It isn't that we've done anything all that exciting, it's just that I have shared the experiences with *him*. He makes everything grander, and I've become addicted to his very presence.

Moonlit walks around the grounds and through the olive groves, and a picnic by a tree-secluded pond. Long and pleasant conversations at an iron bistro table in the courtyard, sipping cold lemonade, as we share personal things about ourselves–our likes and dislikes, what makes us happy or sad, what touches us deep inside. Watching a movie from the large collection of dvds on the massive flat screen television in the media room. Taking a long walk to the other side of the island and getting caught in the rain, then running back to the house, completely soaked to the skin when we reach it. Laughing and shivering at the same time as we track water through the house to go and change, though *I* am the only one shivering since he is immune to the cold. Lacing hot chocolate with extra chocolate to go with the marshmallows we roast over the fire pit out back, which we then sandwich between two chocolate-covered biscotti for our Italian version of smores. It has been a very full two days and he has been true to his word. I have not been bored a single minute.

I smile as I think of this. As of right now, I would have to say Italy is the most perfect place in the world. So what if I haven't seen anything but this island? For right now it is enough. Looking across the table at him, he is smiling as well and I can feel him in my thoughts. When my branded palm begins to tingle, I can briefly hear his thoughts too, and what I hear warms me to the core.

He takes another bite of his chicken. "Another week and you will be a master Italian chef."

"I highly doubt that," I say, laughing. "But I have enjoyed learning to cook different things. I usually have microwave oven dinners because it's no fun just cooking for myself."

"I'm glad I am able to contribute in your culinary enjoyment."

"I am as well." I can't help glancing over at him every now and again. Before meeting him, the only faces I ever saw across the dinner table on a regular basis were the elderly residents at work. Despite the situation, it feels good to not be alone. However, I do miss Henry from time to time.

"We will get you another cat one day."

"I look forward to that. I was never much of a pet person until Henry was given to me. As soon as I saw him I fell in love with him and we became completely inseparable. He was a good friend."

"I don't have many feline tendencies, but I hope I am a okay replacement." I snort at his wide grin. "Well, what did he do that I can't?"

"Hmmm, let's see. He liked to snuggle in my lap and let me scratch behind his ears. He followed me around the house and brushed up against my leg when he wanted attention. And he curled up next to me in bed each night and purred softly before falling asleep."

After contemplating this a moment, he gives me a slow smile. "Well, I could snuggle in your lap, but you would no longer have a lap if I did because your legs would probably be crushed." When I giggle he says, "I'm serious. However, I will allow you to scratch behind my ears if you would like, and I can get down on all fours occasionally and brush up against your leg, though that might be a little embarrassing."

He sends me a mental picture of the scene and I laugh out loud. "A cat the size of a great Dane."

"Exactly. But sadly, I cannot curl up beside you at night right now." Pausing, he stares into my eyes a moment. "Maybe one day."

My face grows hot and flushed. I try thinking of something to say to keep up the bantering, but my mind is completely blank. So I just smile and put another bite of food in my mouth, allowing his comment to brand a place in my thoughts, leaving his personal mark on my heart–a mark that I know will never go away.

After we finish eating, I start clearing everything away, looking forward to sitting in front of the fireplace with him and enjoy more relaxing conversation. He starts helping me load the dishwasher, then stops suddenly, a small growl escaping him, completely startling me.

"Is something wrong?"

Standing as still as a statue for another moment, he closes his eyes. "I sense something on the island."

It is only six words, but they are enough to cause my heart to pound violently. "What is it?" My voice is barely a whisper.

Turning to me, he takes my shaking hands in his. "I am going to find out. I need you to lock all the doors. Do not open them or come out no matter what you hear."

"Okay," I manage, gripping his hands tightly. "Please be careful." I would not be able to forgive myself it anything happened to him, especially while protecting me. I would never get over the loss.

He cups my face. "I will come back to you. I promise." When I nod, he reluctantly pulls his hands from mine and leaves. I then quickly run and lock all the doors.

* * *

The warrior silently walks through the trees, his feet making no sound, so light are his steps. Being stealth is as natural to him as breathing. He scans his surroundings, looking for the smallest movement, his ears tuned to pick up the smallest sound. With each step, the evil presence he senses grows stronger, becoming so tangible he can taste its familiar bitterness sinking into his surroundings, polluting the atmosphere of the island.

His eyes quickly zero in on a lone figure moving through the trees.

"*Ciao*, my friend," the boatman calls and stops.

"*Ciao*." He eyes the man a moment. "Why are you here?"

"I came to warn you. There was someone at Cella's place asking questions."

"What kind of questions?"

"He asked if anyone had seen you, and if so, if you were alone."

"How did you know it was me he was asking about?"

"No one, myself included, knows your name. He asked about 'the ancient one.' No one knew who he was talking about."

"No one except you." The warrior steps closer, every nerve in his body coiled and ready, for he knows the creature he faces, sensing the evil behind the facade. The red aura surrounding the Urchin shines like a beacon. To the human eye it looks just like a man, and many a human is in mortal danger when it is near because they have no clue of its true nature.

"You should not have come."

"I needed to warn you."

"You think to warn me against yourself?"

For a moment, there is silence. Then, as expected, the Urchin sheds the boatman's body like a snake shedding its skin, revealing its true self.

"She must die," it declares in its normal gravelly voice.

"The prophecy will be fulfilled," the warrior declares, readying himself for the oncoming attack.

The Urchin charges forward at lightning speed, but the warrior's reflexes are even quicker. To the human eye, his movements would be undetectable. In the blink of an eye he leaps into the air, landing softly behind the Urchin. The creature draws a steel blade, turns and swings. The warrior meets the weapon with a sword that he'd simply willed into his hand. The third arm of the Urchin appears holding a metal weapon consisting of a steel handle with a long chain attached to a metal round ball with spikes. The spikes secrete a fatal poison and once it pierces the skin, the foe usually dies instantly.

The warrior knows this because he has encountered it before. As the Urchin swings, the weapon is instantly blocked by an impenetrable gold shield, willed into existence. He uses the same shield to deflect the poisonous venom the Urchin spews from its mouth, causing it to splash in the creature's eyes. It staggers back, momentarily blinded, giving the warrior the diversion he'd needed.

He produces a dagger coated in the venom of a sterengall fish–a deadly creature created by Lord Derth, himself–and adds a strong current of electricity before plunging it into the Urchin's heart. It falls to the ground, squirming against the cobbled walkway a moment before turning to ash and disintegrating.

Heaving a deep sigh, the warrior immediately does a complete scan of the island, feeling a profound sadness for the loss of the boatman's life and grateful Lord Derth hasn't done nearly as much damage as he could. He could have murdered or enslaved countless humans during his existence. Instead, the dark lord's efforts have been concentrated on keeping the prophecy from coming to pass.

Quickening his movements, he covers every part of the island. He doesn't think there is another assassin close by because that's not the way Urchins work. Their leader is as arrogant as he is dangerous, assuming it will only take one Urchin to do the job. Still, he is unwilling to take any chances. Celine's life is too important to allow even the smallest risk.

Six

My protector hasn't come back yet and I am worried. No, I'm way past worried. Pacing back and forth in the living room, I repeatedly peek through the curtains for some sign of his return. My heart aches and I feel physical pain as my imagination runs wild, torturing me.

I don't know what I'll do if anything has happened to him. He has only been in my life for a few days, but I feel as if I have always known him. I mean, sure I still don't know his name, but that doesn't matter. He came for me, to protect me and keep me safe. For the first time ever, I know my life has importance, but it will mean nothing without him.

Forcing myself to sit in the large leather chair, I wrap my arms around my middle, trying to stop my hands from shaking, longing for comfort. My eyes drifting, I again take in my surroundings.

Various floral arrangements in tall painted vases are placed around the room and a colorful throw is draped over the arm of the tan corded sofa. A large elegant area rug covers the middle of the tiled floor. Crystal gondola figurines in various sizes sit on the mantle above the fireplace, and a large, gilt-framed mosaic painting hangs on each wall beside painted masks. Like the rest of the house, the room has an understated elegance that is both comforting and inviting.

Until tonight, I have enjoyed the beauty of the house. I've enjoyed it because I have been sharing it with him. Without him it would not be the same.

Please come back to me, I silently plead. *You promised you would come back to me.*

Leaning forward, I close my eyes, pressing my face in my hands, praying he will return soon unharmed. From the moment he walked out the door, I've felt more alone than I ever have before, and every moment he is gone, my pain and fear increases.

I am fine, cara.

His voice suddenly flows into my mind, causing a slow warmth to pierce my fear. I feel him drawing near.

The sound of the front door unlocking momentarily startles me. Then it opens and his voice is caressing my name. In the next moment, I am wrapped in his arms. I cling to him tightly, never wanting to let him go.

"I was so worried," I whisper against his chest.

"I am unharmed," he murmurs, leaning down, pressing his face into my hair. "No matter what, I will always come back to you, and I will always keep you safe."

Heaving a deep sigh, I soak in his warmth, taking comfort in the strength of his muscular body.

After another moment, he draws back. "We will need to move to another safe place."

"When?" I ask, disappointed. I have grown to love the island so.

"Tomorrow evening. I prepared another place, just in case we needed it."

Releasing another weary sigh, I nod, accepting that he knows what is best. "I'll pack some things." I give him a slight smile. "I am definitely taking at least half that wardrobe up there."

Smiling, he presses a warm hand to my cheek. "I thought you would."

Closing my eyes, I lean into his touch. He wraps his other arm around me, holding me close, and I sigh, soaking in his comfort. Against my will, a tear trickles down my face.

I am emotionally weary but relieved he is unharmed, and happy he is here, holding me. Overflowing gratitude makes me treasure the steady sound of his heart beating against my ear. I know he senses my unsteady emotions.

"Come, *cara*," he says, leading me to the sofa. "You are tired and weary. Let me hold you a while."

I sit down next to him and he covers me with the throw, wrapping me in his arms. *Rest. Just rest*, he whispers to my mind. As soon as his lips make contact with my brow, my eyes close and I drift off.

* * *

The warrior mentally revives the dying flames in the fireplace and then closes his eyes, burying his face in her hair. He hadn't expected the Urchin to find them so fast and there can only be one explanation. Evidently someone in his network has turned and is now working for the enemy. He can no longer trust anyone except his blade brother in the states and a priest in Venice who had once lived among their people and had taken a sacred vow to never reveal the presence of their kind. He must contact the two men immediately and inform them that there is a dissenter in the ranks.

Until they can discover who that dissenter is, he can trust no one with the knowledge of their whereabouts. He is completely on his own.

Continuing to hold her in silence, he lets his mind drift back to the year 1310. He had turned twenty and was beginning his training to be the guardian of the Woman of Prophecy. From birth, he was taught of the prophecy and the marvelous changes that would take place as the result of its fulfillment.

He had been deeply honored to be chosen for such a vital and coveted calling. It would be dangerous and he may even lose his life, but dying in defense of the Woman of Prophecy was a risk and an honor many warriors longed to take upon themselves. And *he* had been chosen to be her protector.

He had known there was a great possibility that his *Ki Talimai* would emerge, as would the mark of his bond mate, and he would not be there to accept the bond. This would be painful, but it was necessary, and a sacrifice he'd been willing to make. For he knew that to selfishly reject this calling would not only bring the label of coward upon him, causing him to feel shame among the men of his kind, but if the *Ki Talimai* of his mate called to him and he abandoned his calling to go to her, he and the woman would never be happy, and the bond would weaken and fall apart, destroying them both.

No, he had accepted the honor with humility and gladness.

Training twelve hours a day, he honed not only his fighting skills, he also learned to use and control his growing powers and abilities. Centuries of physical conditioning in both training and battle have prepared him for the enemy he now faces.

He smiles, remembering the day of Celine's birth. Unseen, he had been there, watching over her, ready to protect her from the enemy. Through the years he remained close, watching her grow and witnessing her joys, her sorrows, her triumphs and trials. He'd felt proud of her for the person she was and the great woman she was becoming.

Then two years ago something happened. The mark of the soul's bond burned into his palm like wax melting against a flame. He had wondered how it could be, but he soon discovered that the closer he was to Celine, the more the mark burned. The burning was not painful, but rather comforting, for through it, his mind gained absolute clarity and her thoughts instantly lay open to him. The pull of his soul to hers was immediate, as was her owning of his heart. There have been a few cases in the past in which one of his kind was bound to a regular human. When the blood of the two merged during the final binding ceremony through the ceremonial cut on the wrist, the blood of the human changed and the person became immortal like his kind. When that happened, the two souls permanently merged and became one, and because of this, neither mate could survive without the other.

The moment Celine's soul called to his, the knowledge of his true part in the prophecy flowed into his being, ingraining him with priceless truth and wisdom, giving him answers to internal questions that had burned in his heart for centuries. These realizations filled him with tearful humility and absolute unmeasurable joy. To discover that the Woman of Prophecy and his bond mate were one and the same was more than he could have ever hoped for.

All that he is belongs to her. Always has, and always will.

The fates have been kind.

Seven

Scanning the room once more, I decide I have everything I need. I am zipping up the last of the three large suitcases when my protector enters the bedroom that had briefly belonged to me. The thought of abandoning it renews my sadness. It is strange to feel so attached to this place when my life had been threatened here. But I quickly remind myself that this is not a vacation, that I'm literally running for my life and his job is to protect me. Being with him has allowed me to briefly forget that at times.

"I have what I need," I tell him. I can tell by his expression he is just as sad about having to leave the beautiful island. In the brief time we've been here, we have created some wonderful memories, but I will take them with me, and I know he will as well. He presses a gentle hand to my cheek.

"We will begin again and make new memories."

I smile. "I know."

Somehow he grabs all three suitcases and I follow him out, pausing to take everything in one last time. He locks up the house and we begin our walk down the cobbled path through the tree tunnel. When we reach the dock, he helps me into the boat, then puts my luggage in, placing it next to a couple of boxes he'd loaded earlier. He starts the engine and steers away from the island.

Venice is so beautiful at night. The city is alive with festive lighting, making the elegant old buildings stand out even more. The city lights shine on the water, reflecting off the ripples like precious gems, and though the smell of sulfur is strong, my nose is growing used to it.

It isn't long before we enter a darkened area of the waterfront and pull up next to a dock behind a palace of apartments.

"This is it," he says, his eyes on me as I silently take everything in.

I gaze up at the massive set of wooden doors. Above them are terraced windows and I am anticipating seeing the inside of our new residence. Not knowing for sure how long we will be here, I tell myself not to get too attached.

But once we enter the grand pillared foyer, I immediately fall in love with the place. The apartment has four bedrooms, three bathrooms, two salons, an elegant dining room, a modern kitchen, and a laundry room. Richly decorated, most of the furniture looks antique. Though I will still miss the seclusion of the island, this home speaks comfort and I'm glad to be here.

After bringing everything in, my protector leaves me to unpack while he scans the area surrounding the building. The room I choose has a balcony overlooking a private courtyard in the back. The room next to mine is identical and I am certain he will choose to sleep there in order to remain close to me. I put my clothes, cosmetics and toiletries away. Having finished, I walk over to the balcony doors and stare out into the night. The stars are veiled and the sky is thickly overcast. It looks like we are due for more rain sometime soon.

Heaving a tired sigh, I ponder the danger still looming before me. Something is after me and I still don't fully understand why. He tells me I'm important in some way, that there is something I am supposed to accomplish. And someone is after me, trying to prevent me from doing whatever it is I'm meant to do. In some ways I prefer the mundane days I had before.

But I would never trade being with him. Even if I could go back to my life before, I wouldn't. Not if it meant I would be separated from him. However, I am tired of running and I hope we can stay put for a while. Maybe I should ask him to teach me to fight so I can at least try to protect myself if the enemy should happen to find me when he is not here. Of course, I have no clue of what to even expect. Still, it wouldn't hurt to be a little prepared.

Sitting down on the bed, I pull out my wallet and stare at a photo of my parents. It had been taken a few months before my mother died. She'd lost all her hair from the chemotherapy treatments and was wearing a wig styled in a chic bob. She'd also lost a great deal of weight and was too thin, however, she was still beautiful. Her light brown complexion was flawless, her features perfect. She had a smile that literally lit up the world and was completely contagious. Though my father was also thin from weight loss due to his health, he was tall and handsome, his skin tone matching my mother's. They were always considered an attractive couple by friends and acquaintances.

I lightly run my finger across the photo. Sadly this is the only picture I brought of them and I cherish it immensely.

What would my parents think of my life right now? Mama told me frequently throughout my life that I was special and destined to do great things in the world. Thinking on this, part of me wonders if she knew about this somehow. Or was it just a mother's wishful thinking? Unless she could see into the future, it was most likely the latter.

I really miss my mother at the moment, and I wish she was here to talk me through all of this somehow. Knowing her, she would demand that my protector tell me everything immediately. The thought makes me smile. As loving and giving as she was, patience was never her strong suit.

Looking at the photo once more, I close my wallet and put it back in my purse. My mother may not be here, but I can handle this. I will make it through whatever comes because I have no choice. Hearing the apartment door opening, I rise, going to him.

He smiles, but I sense his deep concern for my safety. I can feel the subtle anguish he harbors at the thought of me being harmed and it affects me deeply. As sudden tears spring to my eyes, I blink them back. Saying nothing, he simply opens his arms and I enter them, soaking in the warmth and safety of his embrace.

* * *

He senses she is hurting and it tears at his heart. He wishes he could offer her more comfort and longs to assure her that there will be no more running, that things will be different. How he wishes he hadn't had to uproot her from her life. Aching to give her the security of a home of her own, he hopes he can sometime in the future. She deserves all the happiness this world has to offer, and he will move heaven and earth to give her that happiness. Anything he can do, he will.

It has always been this way, even when she was young. When she was sick, he would quietly sit by her bed at night, watching over her. And before she awakened, he would slip away, leaving her with a kiss on the forehead and a doll or stuffed animal. If she fell and hurt herself, he would breeze by undetected, taking the pain away with a light touch. When someone hurt her feelings and made her sad, he would softly whisper to her of her worth and how much she is loved. When she lost her parents and felt alone, he was near, aching for her, wishing he could hold her.

But when his *Ki Talimai* appeared, his ache for her changed from that of comfort to one of need–a need burning inside him that only the emotional connection of his true mate would assuage.

Pulling his thoughts back to the present, he feels her trembling and tightens his embrace, wishing he could pull her into himself and shelter her forever. Drawing back a little, he takes in her beautiful, fatigued features.

"You are tired," he says, touching her face. When she nods he scoops her up in his arms and carries her to her room, placing her on the bed.

"Thank you," she says, giving him a sleepy smile.

"You're welcome." He squeezes her hand, hating to be away from her even for a moment. "Sleep well."

"You, too."

Reluctantly leaving her, he moves through the apartment, turning off all the lights. Walking into the salon, he sits in a chair in front of the terrace window and stares out into the night, searching for danger or strange movement of any kind. Reaching out with his senses, he scans for anything that could do Celine harm. Sensing nothing, he leans back in the chair, settling himself for the night, keeping a vigilant watch. He can sense Celine sleeping peacefully now and will let nothing disturb her rest.

Eight

Emerging from a night filled with indescribably disturbing dreams, I awaken to the delicious scent of bacon, eggs and fresh baked pastry.

I inhale deeply, trying to chase away the frightening images. Images of death and bloodshed. Images of people being trampled and murdered by inhuman assailants with the single goal of destroying mankind. Mangled bodies of children littering the streets. Men and women chained together, tattered and broken, reduced to slavery. Smoky surroundings filled with the screams of pregnant women as babies are ripped from their wombs, and the cries of men as they watch helplessly through lifeless eyes the acts of desecration committed on their spouses.

Buildings that were once so tall and beautifully elegant, demolished and crumbling to the ground. Cities becoming barren wastelands. Animals and wildlife destroyed, never again to grace the earth's surface. Trees and plants withering and completely devoid of life. It was as if the world no longer had a soul, like all the life had been completely drained from it.

But worst of all, and the most painful, were images of my protector's body lying in the street along with several others of his kind–his unseeing eyes staring up from a frozen, pain-contorted face, and all breath depleted from his body.

Sitting up, I shudder, doing my best to put the dreams out of my mind, but I know the last image will stay with me. I get up, and taking a set of clean clothes from from the dresser, head to the bathroom to shower.

Closing my eyes, I stand under the water as steam surrounds me and fogs up the glass, wishing the water could somehow wash away the mental picture of him lying lifeless, never again to take me in his arms and warm me in his embrace. Never again to hear him whisper *cara* against my temple or feel his lips brush my brow. The thought of losing him is physically painful, and soon hot tears mingle with the water. Suddenly all the emotions I've kept in control erupt at once and I begin to sob. Pressing my head against the shower wall, I release them all, losing track of time as wrenching, water-muffled sobs wrack my body. I tell myself I have to be strong, not only for me, but for *him*. The last thing he needs is a basket case on his hands. I don't want to be any more of a burden to him than I already am.

Finally exhausting myself, I get a hold of my emotions, mentally promising that I will never break down this way again. I shampoo my hair, rinse my face a final time, and get out. After drying off, I brush through my hair, braid it, and pin it up in a bun, giving up trying to tame the stray curls that fall onto my forehead. I quickly dress and put my things away before joining him.

My protector is sitting at the food-laden table in the dining room, staring out the window, seeming lost in thought. When I enter, he smiles and stands to help me with my chair, seating me next to him. I thank him, marveling anew at how gentlemanly he is.

"You did not rest easy last night," he states, sitting back down.

I should have known he would sense my emotions even while sleeping. It makes me wonder if he slept at all.

"Not last night," he says.

I take in his concerned expression. "The dreams were bad–the worse I have ever had."

"I know." He takes my hand in his, squeezing firmly.

"There was so much violence, so many lives lost, and such terrible destruction. And . . ." My voice breaks off as my eyes travel to his face and I furiously blink back the tears. "And then I saw you . . ."

"Shhh," he soothes. "Do not think on it anymore. Let your mind be at ease, *cara.*"

"But it's almost as if the dreams were some sort of premonition of things to come. Like this is what will be." I look into his eyes, my own imploring. "Is it?"

Closing his eyes, he lifts my hand to his mouth, holding it against his lips.

* * *

The memory of the gruesome images in her dreams causes him to shudder inward. Some of the scenes are familiar to him because he has seen them before in his own dreams. He supposes this is why he hardly sleeps anymore–not that he believes the things of their dreams will come to pass. But it is a possible future–possible but not probable if the prophecy is fulfilled–*when* the prophecy is fulfilled.

He'd felt the anguish she experienced in the shower, had experienced every shudder, felt the trail of each tear that rolled down her face, and it hurt his heart.

Pressing her warm palm to his face, he feels her hand trembling. "Those images are not in our future, Celine. I promise you, I will do everything in my power to keep it from happening." He wants more than anything to pull her close and kiss the worry from her face, but he can't let himself. If he were to kiss her now, the moment his lips should make contact with hers, the burning passion of his immortal soul would take over and he would be unable to stop himself from claiming her body as his own. Until their bond is completed in ceremony, this is something he cannot allow to happen.

* * *

Easier said than done. Making a grand effort, I again try to push my fears aside and hold onto his promise. Allowing my gaze to roam over each feature of his handsome face, my eyes soon travels down to his muscular arms and chest, making the longing to have them passionately wrapped around me and his mouth pressed against mine grow with each passing second. This time, instead of trying to push my emotions away, I fully embrace them, feeling a powerful longing emanating from him as well.

Our time will soon come. His voice fills my mind, his emotions coming through with absolute clarity.

He releases my hand and I finally drop my gaze to the table, taking in the wonderful breakfast he prepared. "Everything looks great. Thank you for cooking."

"You're very welcome. I decided I need to do my part in the kitchen as well and give you a break."

"I really have enjoyed cooking for you. Plus, it's been fun learning new dishes." I pull apart a fluffy croissant. "Please tell me you didn't make these from scratch. They're too perfect."

"Would it make you feel better if I told you I've made them countless times before?"

"A little."

"All right. I have had centuries of practice making them. My mother taught me."

"Well, kudos to your mom. These are delicious."

"Thank you."

"Do you miss your parents?"

He pauses a moment before answering. "Sometimes more than others."

"Do they still live?"

"Yes. I hope to introduce you to them one day."

I smile warmly. "I hope for that as well. So, where exactly do your kind live? I mean, surely you didn't come from another planet." I almost laugh at the absurdity.

"Our survival depends on the secrecy of the location of our home. I cannot tell you now for your own protection, as well as that of my people. But hopefully one day soon you will see it for yourself."

Nodding in acceptance, I again remind myself that every decision he makes is for my welfare.

"Do you have any siblings?"

"No, there is just me. Maybe one day my parents will be blessed with another child."

"When I was young I wished for a brother or sister, but Mama was only able to have me. Health problems shattered her dreams of ever having another baby. They were always pretty protective of me, probably because if anything happened to me, that would be the end of our bloodline. When I was older, my parents told me they couldn't have any more children and I was sad, but they showered me with all the love they could and I lacked for nothing. I was a happy child. Happy and very fortunate to have them as parents."

"And they were fortunate to have you." He squeezes my hand in comfort and affection.

We finish eating and I help him clear everything away. Leaving the kitchen, I enter the front salon and gaze through the terrace window down into the rippling water. There are water buses cruising back and forth, delivering passengers to their various destinations. I marvel at how oblivious the citizens and tourists are to the evil surrounding them— clueless of the hidden element that lies awake in the dark alleyways of the city, waiting to wreak destruction on the human soul. Shuddering, I rub the goosebumps on my arms and try to replace the disturbing thoughts with something else.

I feel his presence even before he touches me and I sigh as his muscular arms come around me, holding me close. He clearly senses my inner distress. I soak in the comfort he gives.

"Will you tell me about your home, what it's like?"

Tightening his embrace slightly, he leans down and rests his head against mine. There is a melancholy tone to his voice when he speaks.

"It is very green, and the colors of the flowers, trees, and the sky are more vivid than you could possibly imagine." He moves his face to my hair. "The sounds of birds, the smell of nature, the taste of food. It is all blissfully intoxicating. Our cottages are large and comfortable, and we have everything we need or want. There is no war, no violence there. Everyone lives in peace."

"It sounds Utopian," I murmur in wonder.

"Not Utopian, but more heavenly than I can describe. We work for what we have. We reap only what we sow. We get out only what we put into our way of life. We strive to be kind and fair, to love our neighbor, and we do what we can to help those we share this world with. This is very important to us. But we also stand ready to defend our home, our children, family, loved ones, and our lives."

Turning in his arms, I raise my eyes to his, letting my gaze travel over his angelically handsome features. "You are a great people and this world is blessed by your presence." I caress his face. "I know *I* am."

His piercing gaze captures mine. "Do you truly feel that way? Are you truly happy to be with me?"

Staring into his imploring eyes, tears rise in mine. *How can you doubt it? Can you not feel it? Just look into my eyes. Can you not see it?*

He lifts a warm hand to my cheek. "*Si, cara,*" he whispers huskily. "I see it." Taking my hand, he presses it against his chest. "I feel it." His embrace tightens as he pulls me further into himself.

His words wash over me, through me, making me never want to leave this spot, or ever be away from him. We stand for a while in silence, each of us lost in our own thoughts.

After a long while I finally ask, "What does 'cara' mean?" I have wanted to ask him for some time now but have been too shy to.

Touching his lips to my ear, he whispers, "It means beloved."

The sensation and heady sound of his words causes a blissful shiver to move through me. "*Cara,*" I whisper, testing the word in my own voice. The one word says so much to me, and the warmth I experience each time he uses

74

it to address me is now magnified. This one word conveys what he is not yet free to say. I feel this with absolute certainty and marvel at how strongly my heart answers.

Our time will soon come, he tells me again and I hold to his words.

* * *

It rains on and off throughout the day, but I am somehow comforted by the sound. The temperature has dropped outside and it is a bit chilly, but I am warmed, not only by the house, but by the company as well.

We share a picnic dinner on the floor by the fireplace in the inner salon. It is a simple meal of panini sandwiches, salad, and chocolate cheesecake. The cheesecake is a recipe handed down from my mother. I had enjoyed making it again. Each bite brings me a bit of home.

Afterward, wrapped in a quilt, I curl up next to him and we silently gaze into the flames. The sun set long ago and now the light from the fire dances against the walls of the darkened room. Relaxed with my head resting against his chest, his soothing heartbeat causes a feeling of languidness to envelop me. At night, his warmth is always like a sedative, and I fall asleep easily in his embrace.

Feeling him shift, I awaken just as he lifts me in his arms. He pauses a moment, holding me close. Sometimes it's like I am being embraced by a giant. I guess in a sense, I *am.*

Even at six feet, I feel positively short around him. I wrap my arms around his neck as he carries me to my room, feeling as secure as a child, yet his touch elicits womanly responses. He places me on the bed.

"Goodnight, *cara*," he breathes, pressing a kiss to my brow.

I smile sleepily. "Goodnight."

His look is one of mutual longing as he closes the door.

* * *

Reaching out with his mind, the warrior checks the doors and windows, making sure they are locked. He turns off the light, again positioning himself in front of the terrace window, and stares out into the night. The rain has increased and is falling hard. He listens to the patter of large drops hitting the roof and landing against the window.

He is restless tonight, even more so than normal. Closing his eyes, he takes a calming breath, then slips into meditation. It is effortless for him to become one with the earth and the elements. He learned at an early age how to merge his soul with nature, being taught that the earth is a living breathing thing with a spirit. All the people of his kind have this gift. However, he is even more gifted, and his ability to commune with nature and his surroundings is especially strong. He can hear the wind as it speaks to the atmosphere and the atmosphere's submission in this partnership called weather. He can see and feel the exact size and shape of each raindrop that falls–the pattern of each snowflake that drifts softly to the ground in the winter, and the ferociousness of a tornado as it touches down, destroying everything in sight. He knows the elements intimately and respects them all.

Continuing to listen to the rain, he begins to relax, his body slowly growing languid, one organ and limb at a time.

* * *

A moment later the warrior's eyes snap open, and in a flash he is in Celine's room, startling the creature before it had had time to draw a blade. His heart lurches, instant fury filling him as the Urchin snatches Celine up and sprints through the balcony doors with her clutched in its claws. Releasing an inhuman roar of rage, he lunges through the doors into the rain, staying right on the creature's tail.

Celine's body is limp. Reaching out with his mind, he assesses her condition. She has been injected with an Urchin sedative, most likely to keep her from fighting or screaming should she had awakened, but she is otherwise unharmed, for which he is humbly and gratefully surprised. Something tells him the Urchin's orders have changed and Lord Derth wants his minion to bring her to him alive, otherwise she would be dead now. Maybe he wants the satisfaction of killing her himself. That would be like him and it's the only explanation the warrior can think of.

He trails the Urchin as it weaves back and forth through alleyways, trying to lose him, but the creature's efforts are in vain. Finally, it stops in front of St. Mark's Basilica.

Standing a few yards away from the creature, preparing for battle, he watches it hurls Celine toward the building wall. He sends out a powerful strand of air, catching her before she hits the hard surface, and gently places her on the pavement by the church doors. Then he turns and faces the creature.

In an instant, both leap into the air towards one another, the warrior wielding a sword and shield, the Urchin holding poisonous daggers. He manages to deflect every dagger, destroying each blade that hits his shield. He swings his sword toward the creature's head and the Urchin blocks the blade with its own.

Thus the hour-long battle begins.

Nine

The Present

Tightening his embrace, my protector holds me closer. Everything about him is familiar to me. He exudes peace, safety, and comfort, and being with him is home. I press my face in the curve of his neck, wanting to curl up inside him and never move.

Tonight I was closer to death than ever before, and I had been completely unaware of it. For that, I am grateful. I caught a glimpse of the creature before it injected me, and even though it was only for a fraction of a second, the hideous sight will stay with me forever.

But what is it? And why does it want to kill me?

It is time, cara. *I will tell you everything.*

Lifting my eyes to his face, I give him my full attention. He draws back, taking my hands in his. "My name is Sebastian. Sebastian Giovanni."

"Sebastian," I whisper. It thrills me to finally know his name, to be able to say it. "So you really are Italian?"

"Technically, yes. I was born in Italy. My parents decided to leave our real home, Challis, before I was born and moved to Venice. We lived here for my first nineteen years. Gideon, the man you met who helped us get here, is my cousin. He moved to the surface in 1798." My mouth forms an o at finally knowing a little more about the blond man. Sebastian continues. "Our height caused my parents and me to stick out like sore thumbs. By my nineteenth birthday, my parents missed our home and moved back so I could begin my training. Every young man of my kind begins his training at twenty and hopes to be given the calling of protector. I was blessed to be chosen. "

"Chosen for what?"

"To be the protector of the Woman of Prophecy." He squeezes my hand. "It is you, Celine. You are the Woman of Prophecy."

Woman of Prophecy? My mouth moves, but nothing comes out, and my mind is exploding with questions, but I press my lips together, allowing him to continue.

"When we are young, we are taught that one day there would be born to this earth a woman who will bear a golden son, a child whose birth would end the reign of Lord Derth, the leader of the Urchins. It has been foretold that the child's very birth will incinerate him and all who follow him instantly. They will turn to dust where they stand. He will possess the purest spirit to ever be born to this earth. When he draws his first breath, the enemy will draw his last."

My heart is pounding like crazy. "Me? Give birth to a golden child? How is this possible?"

"You were chosen long before you came into this life. *The One* chose you, and he chose me to be your protector. But more than that, I am your true mate in every way."

As he says this, I look at my hand, noticing the painless burning of the mark. Placing his open palm over mine, I gasp as heat ignites between us, traveling from my head to my feet.

I have no idea how all of this is happening or why it's happening to *me*. I only know that it is–and it makes complete and perfect sense. I look up into his eyes as he closes his hand around mine and the heat becomes a steady burn, consuming me.

Falling in love with him has never been an option, for my heart has been there from the first. It is real, it is powerful, and it is making itself known with force. Looking into my eyes, he unleashes his innermost thoughts. I am instantly hit with the blinding force of his feelings and the rush is staggering.

Raising my branded hand to his face, tears fill my eyes, spilling down my cheeks, and the words come easy. "I love you, Sebastian," I whisper. His eyes grow misty as well.

"And I love you, Celine. I always have." He caresses my face, wiping a tear away. "Will you take vows with me and complete our bonding through ceremony?"

"Yes," I whisper, almost too choked up with emotion to speak. This beautiful and amazing immortal is going to be mine! He wants to bind himself to *me*! I can scarcely take in the enormity of it all. Not that I haven't dreamed about having full claim of him, but to know it will really happen just blows me away. But a thought quickly occurs to me.

"Sebastian, I am mortal, but you aren't. You will live forever and I . . ."

"Shhh," he soothes. "Do not fear, *cara*, for during the ceremony my blood becomes yours, and yours mine, making us one. You will become one of us." His gaze caresses my face. "And you will truly be mine in every way."

"I will become one of you?"

"You will." He turns to the priest standing against the door. "*Padre*, the ceremony, please."

Glancing down at myself, I notice for the first time the white gown I am wearing. *How . . .*

Before I can even finish the thought, Sebastian mentally voices the answer. *I have many powers I have kept hidden. Now I can share them with you. And it will be my privilege to help you learn to use your new abilities as well.*

I can only shake my head in wonder, certain that I will be doing a lot of that. I watch the priest as he removes a painting from the wall that had concealed a safe. Opening the safe he removes an old, intricately carved wooden box. He opens it and pulls out three wrapped objects, uncovering each one. One is a wooden scroll that looks ancient. The second, a silver knife with a jeweled handle, and the last, a silver and gold-twined rope. Startled by the knife, I feel Sebastian soothing my emotions.

"This is the ceremonial dagger used to bind our blood, and on the scroll is written the Challissian Bonding Prayer." He smiles at the priest. "Father Battiano is a friend of our people and was chosen for this very purpose."

I look at the holy man and he smiles, bowing. Placing the scroll and dagger on a small rolling table, he moves it to my beside.

"Celine," Sebastian says softly, "we have less time than I had hoped and we must perform the ceremony now. Then we must leave and return to my people. Once we are bonded, Challis in the only place you will truly be safe. Lord Derth has no knowledge of the location of our home. When we reach my world, neither he nor his minions will ever find us."

We must move again. Of course I knew it was inevitable, but I didn't realize it would be so soon. Sighing, I nod in acceptance.

He touches my face. "I promise, when we reach Challis, you will have a home and we will never have to run again."

I smile, covering his hand with mine, knowing he speaks the truth.

He nods to the priest to begin. Joining hands, our gazes are locked as the ceremonial words are read. Since they are written in the language of Sebastian's people, he telepathically translates them for me.

"Sebastian, do you accept Celine as your true mate, in heart, mind, body, soul, and blood, for the eternities and beyond all time?"

"Ki," he answers with strength in his own language.

"Celine, do you accept Sebastian as your true mate, in heart, mind, body, soul, and blood, for the eternities and beyond all time?"

"Ki," I answer fervently.

The priest binds our arms together with the rope. He takes the dagger, and with a swift stroke, runs the blade across our skin, then presses our arms together, pulling the rope tighter.

I suck in a breath. It had been so quick, the cut didn't have time to hurt, and his blood mixes with mine immediately. Like a bullet from a gun, it courses through my system and heat spreads over my whole body. My skin tingles, my senses sharpening to the point of overload. I sway a little and feel Sebastian's arms come around me.

"Are you all right, beloved?"

Squeezing my eyes shut, I shake my head a little. His angelic voice is so much richer to my ears. I open my eyes, taking him in with renewed awe. He is much more beautiful than I'd realized.

"I'm all right," I finally answer. He smiles, letting his eyes roam over my face.

It is I who did not think you could be any more beautiful. I was mistaken.

I wish I had a mirror to see myself, to see what he is seeing, but that will have to wait. He stares at me another moment before nodding to the priest to continue.

The holy man returns to the safe and pulls out a folded white cloth before heading into the small bathroom. I hear him turn on the faucet. He returns and unties the rope before rubbing the cloth over our arms and I gasp again. Both cuts have completely healed. I raised my eyes to

Sebastian again in renewed wonder, the urge to wrap my arms around him and crush my lips to his so strong that I almost can't breathe. The same emotions emanate from him, heating my entire body, and it's all I can do not to melt in a puddle at his feet. The clearing of the priest's throat pulls me back to the moment. When I turn to see him smiling, I suddenly wonder if he can read my mind as well.

No, my beloved sends to me. *But he can read your face.*

Feeling my cheeks warm, I give the priest my attention once more and Sebastian again translates.

"Two have now become one. Two bodies have become one flesh. He is your husband. She is your wife. The bond is complete and your lives are forever tied."

Sebastian smiles, and instead of kissing my lips, kisses my hand. I am royally disappointed until I hear his voice in my mind, the tone of it hoarse and full of yearning.

I dare not trust myself to kiss you just yet for fear of losing control and crossing boundaries that should not be crossed until we are alone.

My face growing hot, I silently concur.

He turns to the priest. "Thank you, my friend."

"I am deeply honored to have been blessed with the privilege of binding the Woman of Prophecy to her true mate. This has indeed been the greatest thing I have ever, or will ever do in my life."

Sebastian smiles, clasping his hand. "It is we who are honored to have your friendship. We will treasure it well."

The priest nods, then cleans the dagger and rolls up the scroll before placing all the items back in the wooden box and returning it to the safe. Replacing the painting, he accompanies us out to the main door. He places a hand on Sebastian's shoulder.

"Please take care and have a safe journey. Be watchful."

"We will," Sebastian assures him.

* * *

The skies are clear as we make our way back to the apartment. I know we will have to leave later this morning, but I will spend these final hours in Venice tangled in the arms of my husband. Holding me securely, he runs swiftly through the dark, his senses ever tuned, seeking lurking danger. The alleyways go by in a blur, giving me no time to wonder if another creature is hiding nearby.

In less than a minute we arrive. When we are inside, he quickly checks every room before securing all doors and windows. When he is finished, he finds me in the middle salon, standing in front of the fireplace, having glimpsed my reflection in the large mirror above the mantle. My brown complexion is fairer, now more tan than brown, my once brown eyes now a vivid shade of hazel and slightly slanted. My trim figure is still trim, but my arms and legs are defined with lean muscle. My hair feels and looks more luxurious, the spiraled curls rich and luminous.

For the first time in my life, I truly *feel* beautiful.

I am also nervous. I don't know why, but I am. Sebastian senses this. Pulling me close, he holds me in his warm embrace. I calm immediately, my nervousness quickly giving way to a totally different feeling. Turning again toward the mirror, we stare at our reflection for a moment, smiling lovingly at one another. His gentle voice breaks the silence.

"Two years ago, I came to understand the part I was destined to have in the prophecy. I felt deeply honored, awed, and blessed. And now that you are my wife, the feeling has increased tenfold."

"It is *I* who am honored," I softly say. "I still feel completely unworthy of this, but I will try to bring honor to you . . . and our people."

He draws back slightly, turning me to face him again, gently taking my face between his hands. "You honor me just by existing, beloved. You honor me by willingly binding your life to mine–by accepting your calling as the Woman of Prophecy." He lowers his face closer to mine. As he whispers the next words, his warm breath brushes against my face and lips, producing a heady rush in me, causing my whole being to tingle.

"You are mine now, beloved, as I am yours. My blood flows through your veins. I now live in you, and you in me."

As soon as his warm mouth makes contact with mine, heat rushes through my entire body and I immediately understand why he couldn't kiss me before. Not only would it have been his undoing, it would have been mine as well, just as it is now. My lips part and he deepens the kiss, his tongue tasting mine. His mouth is moist, sweet, heated, demanding, and fulfilling. Never in my life have I experienced such love, such passion, such desire, such need. And I never will again with anyone but him. I sigh as his mouth sears a burning path down my neck and over my face before finally claiming my waiting lips again, tasting, teasing, feasting, taking my very breath away.

My arms are around him, my hands clutching his shirt. My palms explore the taunt muscles of his back and shoulders, and my body melts into his. I feel so at one with one with him, I can't tell where I end and he begins.

You are mine, beloved. Only mine. His rich, deep voice plays in my head, wreaking blissful havoc on my senses. *Everything I am is yours.* Our kisses become frenzied and desperate, as if any moment could be our final one. His emotional, aching need burns through me and I welcome its mingling with mine. *You are mine. My wife. My love. My heart. My soul. My true mate.* His muscular arms are steel bands that I never wish to escape. *You are mine, Celine. You belong to me. Say it.*

His love and longing penetrate every part of me, and the power of it feeds my own with a voraciousness that is almost frightening. *I am yours!* I tell him. *I am yours. Your wife. Your love. Your heart. Your soul. Your true mate. I belong to you.* Tangling my fingers in the silky strands of his hair, I hold him impossibly closer, feeling his heart pounding madly, matching mine beat for beat.

He parts his lips from mine, lifting me in his arms.

Then Sebastian, the beautiful being who is now my husband, my protector, my guardian, my heart, my soul, my love, and my life, carries me to our room and I give myself to him, melding my body and soul with his, secure in the knowledge that we are indeed now one in all things.

* * *

It is five in the morning, but Sebastian has yet to close his eyes. For to sleep would mean he would no longer be gazing at the woman in his arms, and he just can't take his eyes from her–not yet. His long body is curved around hers, which keeps his legs from hanging off the bed too much. He could have altered the bed, but chose not to. He can be closer to her this way. It is no longer raining and the last remnants of night linger in the room. The light from a distant street lamp shines through the sheer curtains hanging from the half-open bedroom window, casting shadow roses on the wall.

He continues to gaze at his wife's shadowed profile, seeing her as clearly as if it were daylight. His eyes roam over her, taking in the curves of her body through the silky white sheet, clearly seeing the downy soft hair on her exposed arm. Lightly running his hand over the surface, he watches with pleasure her skin's reaction to his touch, the down immediately shifting. His gaze moves back to her face, encountering her beautiful smile. Staring into her eyes, he rubs his thumb over the tiny, black beauty mark beside her mouth, grateful that the change did not take it away. Moving his thumb to her parted lips, he can't resist following it with his own lips. Her mouth is warm and sweet, and completely intoxicating. When she sighs, the sound ripples through him, provoking a returning growl from deep within.

"Am I a suitable replacement for Henry now?" he asks in a raspy voice, drawing a soft laugh from her.

"More than suitable. You're not as furry, but I am willing to compromise."

"That's very kind of you."

"What can I say? I love strays." He purrs against her ear and tickles her, making her jump. She laughs, catching his hand. He watches her trail a finger over his open palm, tracing the lines showing through his *Ki Talimai*, before pressing her own mark against his. The heat is instant and he tightens his fingers around hers, bringing the back of her hand to his lips.

He remembers his father talking with him about what to expect when he was finally bound to his true mate. He told him how much more intense a couple's emotions are toward one another, how even a simple touch would be overwhelming. Because of being chosen to be the guardian of the Woman of Prophecy, he hadn't known if he would ever be gifted with those experiences. But the fates had been kind and his true mate had been placed before him, taking him by complete surprise.

Now, as he lay with her, soaking in her warmth and sharing a bed for the first time in his long life, he fully understands his father's words, completely grasping what he'd meant when he said, "The love you share with your true mate will swallow you whole, son. It is all consuming without beginning or end. You become one another's lifeline. One cannot survive without the other." Oh, how he knows the truth of it! And the reality of her being in danger washes over him anew. He can never let anything happen to her and will protect her with his last breath. For to lose her would not only be the end of the world as they know it, it would be the end of him, too.

He reins in his thoughts, not wanting to upset her in any way, but he cannot disguise the tears now filling his eyes, and he knows she sees them.

Celine lifts a hand to his face, caressing his cheek. Feeling her concern, he quickly replaces the previous thoughts with the consuming love he harbors for her. "You are everything to me, beloved."

Saying nothing, she wraps her arms around him, capturing his mouth with hers. The rush of her emotions wash over him, showing him that no words are needed.

Ten

We travel by private plane to Ellesmere Island, Canada.

Before leaving Venice, Sebastian explained to me that to make sure we were not being followed, we would need to stay mobile for several days. So we flew to Russia, staying one night in Moscow, and from there to Montreal. We rented a cottage there and laid very low. For two days, we simply immersed ourselves in each other, spending our days by the fire wrapped in one another's arms as he told me more about Challis. Our nights were spent by that same fire, making love and creating searing heat of our own. Because the beds were always too short for him and he found altering them a waste of time, we usually slept on the floor, and I laughed when he told me about the beds in Challis being custom made to accommodate his people, both the men and the women, which meant they would most likely swallow me whole. I was looking forward to feeling short around other women for a change.

He spent some time demonstrating a few of his various powers–moving objects, causing things to appear and disappear into thin air, sedating and calming others, dressing and undressing, all with the power of his mind. The last ability saved us both a lot of time, which was very convenient when it came to certain things.

When we finally left the cottage and made it to the airstrip, Sebastian surprised me by saying he would be flying the plane from here on out. It would be safer that way, and we would be changing our mode of transportation on Ellesmere Island.

As we step off the plane onto yet another private airstrip, a black SUV is waiting for us. This tall driver is older, his skin very fair, and his face is one of the kindest I have ever seen. He smiles, bowing slightly before clasping hands with Sebastian.

She is even more beautiful than I imagined she would be, comes the man's voice in my mind.

She is, Uncle, Sebastian agrees.

Uncle? I question.

Yes, cara. He smiles. *Celine, meet my uncle Aaron. Uncle Aaron, I am honored to present my wife, Celine.* His uncle's eyes widen.

The One *truly has guided you with his hand. Your destiny was set from the beginning–to be not only the guardian, but also the true mate of the Woman of Prophecy.* His expression is one of awe.

When the knowledge came to me, I was just as surprised as you are, Uncle, but by that time, my feelings for her were already sealed in stone. Turning to me, he smiles, raising my hand to his lips.

It is good to meet you, Uncle Aaron, I finally relay.

It is indeed an honor and a joy to meet you, and call you family.

I smile, instantly loving the older man.

I get in the vehicle while Sebastian and his uncle put the luggage in the back. Smiling, I contemplate how comfortable I am in the below freezing weather. For the sake of appearances, we had worn coats when we arrived in Canada, but the truth is, we both could have walked the city completely naked and it would have felt like summer. I am definitely loving being immune to the cold.

Sebastian gets in, grinning at the visual he picks up from my thoughts. "The drive is not very far," he tells me, holding my hand between his. Fortunately, he has given me a few lessons in not only telepathically communicating my thoughts, but keeping them closed to others as well. It's a good thing, too, because Uncle Aaron would definitely be blushing right now.

A few minutes later, we pull off the main road and drive down a graveled path into a forest of leafless trees. After another mile or so, the road stops at the edge of a large, grassy clearing. The tall trees form a circle around the area, as if they had been planted this way.

We get out of the car and Sebastian and his uncle grab our luggage. Stand next to the car, I quietly look around. The trees are bare, standing like sentinels around a dormant golfing green. It is totally quiet and the area looks devoid of wildlife. The skies are clear and sunny, despite the cold.

"Come, *cara*," Sebastian says softly.

Giving him a slightly wary smile, I follow. We are supposed to be taking a different mode of transportation for the duration of the trip, but I see nothing with an engine nearby. I silently walk behind the two men. Reaching the edge of the clearing, they stop and Uncle Aaron begins to speak in Chalissian, and finally I understand the words. It is more of a chant really. He says the phrase three times.

Two seconds later there is a rumble beneath the earth. Sebastian reaches for my hand, mentally assuring me that everything is okay. My eyes widen as the circle of ground opens up, the dormant grass neatly parting as two large metal doors swing open beneath it. Ten seconds later, a shiny silver craft rises from the hole. The ground closes and the craft lands on the same spot. It looks like an Air Force B-2 Stealth Bomber plane, only sleeker with a larger cockpit. I have only seen pictures of these kinds of air crafts, but seeing one in real life just blows me away. And that this particular craft is not conventional or the standard Air Force design leaves me even more in awe.

"It's beautiful," I whisper.

"It is," Sebastian agrees. "It is very fast and undetectable to radar, which is important since the secrecy of the location of our home is so vital."

"Where did it come from? I mean, how did you get it?"

"My people designed it." He smiles. "Our technology is far more advanced than the rest of the world. We have achieved much, and someday, when the rest of mankind is ready, we will share our knowledge."

Uncle Aaron grins. "Ready to take a ride, my lady?"

Grinning back, I nod eagerly, feeling like a kid getting ready to go on an amusement park ride, my fear of flying long gone now. Sebastian keeps my hand tucked in his as we approach the plane. It is massive, its surface flawless, like it has just come from the factory. Even from where we are, I can see myself in the mirrored finish.

When we are a few yards away, Sebastian lifts his hand and the door opens. A set of metal steps unfold, touching the ground. He turns to his uncle and the two men embrace. After a moment, the older man releases his nephew and approaches me, taking my hand in his.

"It has truly been an honor."

I smile and hug him, drawing a small gasp of surprise from him. *Thank you for everything, Uncle Aaron. I hope to see you again one day.*

He chuckles, hugging me back. *I hope for that as well.* Releasing me, he smiles at us. "Safe travel to you both. And may *The One* watch over and keep you, that the prophecy might be fulfilled."

"Be safe, Uncle," Sebastian says.

Holding the metal handrail, I board the plane. Sebastian follows me with the luggage.

Eleven

The interior of the craft is luxurious and roomy, the cabin combined with the cockpit. I take a seat in one of the three tan leather chairs while Sebastian stores our bags. Buckling my seat belt, I gaze around the cabin, taking everything in. It has all the comforts of home. The walls are covered with a light maple wood and the carpet is a plush forest green. A square glass table sits between the seats, topped with a few leather-bound books, and there is a white marble counter top with a small sink. A mini stainless steel refrigerator sits underneath. A microwave sits on the counter and the doors on the upper and lower cupboards are glass. One side holds food, the other houses dishes. In the back, an open door exposes an elegant bathroom.

"Boy, you guys definitely like to travel in style."

"We do," Sebastian says. Waving the plane door shut, he comes and kneels by my seat. "Would you like me to get you anything before we take off?"

Smiling, I press a hand to his handsome face. "No, I'm fine."

He turns his head, kissing my palm. "Uncle Aaron has informed the homeland of our coming, so be prepared to be hugged to death by my parents and greatly honored by our people."

"Will we live with your parents?" I ask. If so, I will miss the privacy we've enjoyed.

"No, a home has been prepared for us. I would miss our privacy as well." His sexy smile is wide. "Because of the speed we will travel, we should be in Challis in about an hour."

"Good. I don't think I could stand not being next to you for longer than that."

He leans forward, lightly touching his lips to mine, but it isn't light for long. He kiss turns heated as his warm mouth passionately explores mine, immediately setting my insides on fire. Pulling him closer, he moans as my fingers are buried in his silky hair. His arms band around me and I meet the staggering explosion of his emotions with the hopeless desperation of my own.

Drawing back slightly, he presses his forehead against mine, saying in a raspy, passion-filled voice, "If we stay this way any longer, I fear we won't make it home today."

I smile, and with a great deal of effort, slow my breathing and remove my fingers from his hair. Tucking my hands under my knees, I lock them there, knowing that if I touch him again, we really *won't* reach our destination today.

Brushing his lips against mine once more, he whispers, "I promise you, *cara*, we will take this up again later."

"I'll hold you to that," I breathe, inhaling his scent deeply, letting it fill my lungs. It will have to sustain me until we can be alone again. He stands and I watch him walk to the pilot seat, taking in the way the black leather pants and white shirt fit his perfect physique. Even bending to keep his head from hitting the ceiling, his walk is alluring, graceful and sleek, yet totally masculine, and totally him. He is the most perfect looking man I have ever seen and he is all mine. Heaving a deep sigh, I swallow against my need for him, doing my best to concentrate on something else. I hear his deep chuckle in my mind.

The feeling is very mutual, beloved.

Sighing again, I watch him for another moment as he pushes several buttons on a panel that looks like it's straight from a movie spaceship before turning my gaze to the window. We lift up off the ground and I am surprised because I don't feel it. Once we are clear, the plane zooms forward. It is as if we are standing still, but we are clearly traveling at an incredible speed. The vast icy landscape flies before my eyes, making it impossible to focus on anything, so I don't even try. Instead I pick up one of the leather-bound books. The writing on the front cover is Challissian, and thanks to my new abilities and the blood now flowing through my veins, I am able to read it clearly.

"Ki Kulimek sa Challis." "The Book of Challis."

The book is filled with beautiful pictures of lush green landscapes and grassy fields dotted with the most incredibly colored flowers I have ever seen. Leafy trees in an array of vivid shades fill the forests, and the lakes are crystal clear, exposing the beautiful tropical fish inhabiting them. Mountains merge into clear blue skies and prehistoric looking birds swoop through the air, some grazing in fields of tall grass. There is even a photo of . . . *Are my eyes deceiving me? It couldn't be!* I stare open-mouthed at a photo of a group of woolly mammoths roaming in a countryside! Woolly mammoths! I can't believe it!

I loose track of time looking at the pictures. Page after page is covered in unbelievable nature scenes, each one indescribably beautiful.

"Cara," Sebastian calls, "look out your window."

Pulling my eyes away from the photos, I am stunned speechless by the same beauty outside my window.

I can't believe it! What happened to all the ice and snow? And how can I see land now when I couldn't before?

He answers my mental questions with one of his own. "Did you know there really is no north pole?"

"No?" I answer back and he laughs.

"No. It is because man's idea of the direction of true north is off. There is no true north, or rather there is, but on the globe, true magnetic north is under so-called cloud cover, which is just another product of surface government propaganda. And for that, our people are grateful. You see, we have traveled far, past the polar ice cap and into the earth. Challis, our home, is in the center of the earth."

To say I am incredulous doesn't begin to cut it. "You're kidding! We are in the center of the earth? But how? Shouldn't we have been flying down into darkness or something?"

"The diameter of the earth's opening is ninety miles across. It is so large, you don't know you are flying into the earth's core. Our home is completely undetectable. Despite the ice that surrounds the opening, the temperature here is a comfortable seventy-six degrees. The atmosphere and weather is always perfect, and we even have our own sun."

Finally closing my mouth, I shake my head in wonder. The theory of the earth being hollow has been around for decades, and even the two college professors who swear they have proof of a government cover-up concerning this subject have been dismissed as crackpots.

"And we are grateful they have been," Sebastian says. "What man doesn't seem to understand is that all planets possess a womb, and earth was born from the womb of another larger planet. It is the way *The One* creates solar systems. It's common sense if the natural man would just open his mind and study it. However, as I said, for now we are grateful for the skeptics. The last thing we need is to have people suddenly taking field trips to Challis. Besides needing to keep our existence secret, there are a great many treasures in Challis. Gold, diamonds, and many other gemstones abound in our world, the sight of which would definitely bring out the greed in men. And the enemy would surely have the upper hand if our home were to be discovered."

Thinking on all of this, I too, am very grateful the hollow earth subject is dismissed by the world as just a theory.

Sebastian turns to me, smiling. "Now, as for your second question, you can see land now because we have stopped flying and are just hovering while preparations are being made for our landing."

Looking down, I take in the numerous roadways webbing out into suburbs surrounded by the same mountainous backdrops I studied in the book. "It is too beautiful for words," I whisper.

"It is indeed," he agrees. He turns back to the controls as a voice transmits through the speakers on the panel in Challissian.

"Sir, you are cleared for landing." The tone of the voice is both authoritative and kind.

"Preparing to land," Sebastian says back.

I stare out the window as we begin to descend, marveling that I am actually in the center of the earth! Forget science fiction and fantasy. *I* am really *here.* And it will be my home! I grin and Sebastian chuckles, sensing the giddiness quickly rolling through me.

A tall glass building appears and we land on the roof in the designated spot. I am still amazed that during the entire trip, it never felt like we were moving, and the landing is the same. Sebastian stands and a bit of nervousness creeps into me.

"Are you ready, beloved?" He kneels in front of me, taking my hands.

Looking into his eyes, I know he senses what I'm feeling before I even voice it. "What if I'm not accepted? What if your parents don't like me, or they don't find me worthy enough for the calling of Woman of Prophecy? What if–" He touches a finger to my lips.

"There is no reason to fear any of those things, for you truly *are* the Woman of Prophecy, and you *are* worthy. Everyone who looks upon you will see this and will count themselves blessed to be in your presence. " He raises my hand to his lips. "I will forever be amazed and grateful that I was chosen to be your guardian, that your soul called to mine and we are eternally bound." Moving closer, he touches his lips to mine, whispering, "I am thankful you belong to me and no one else."

He quickly deepens the kiss and calming warmth flows through me. Before the heat grows to inferno temperatures, I draw back, catching my breath. "If you want me to be able to walk off this plane on my own two feet, we had better postpone all kissing until we are in the privacy of our own home."

He grins. "A good suggestion." I finally stand and he again takes my hand as we deplane. A tall, attractive man and woman are waiting at the bottom of the steps. They both smile and there is no question they are Sebastian's parents–

and my new in-laws. When we reach them, he releases my hand and his mother flies into his arms.

Sebastian laughs. "How I have missed you, Mother! And you, too, Father," he adds, turning and embracing his father.

"We've missed you," his mother says. "And we're so glad you are home."

"I am as well."

As they turn to me, the nervousness inches its way back inside. Pushing it down, I offer a trembling smile and Sebastian moves to me, placing a hand on the small of my back. "Mother, Father, may I present my wife, Celine. Celine, these are my parents."

His mother timidly moves forward, taking my hand. "It is indeed an honor. My name is Sarah, but I would be pleased and honored to have you call me Mother."

I smile, taking in her long blond hair, violet eyes, and tanned skin. A foot shorter than her son, she is absolutely beautiful. "I am happy to meet you, and I would love to call you mother." Her grin is so wide, I can't help grinning in return, and I give into the urge to hug her, warmed as she happily accepts my embrace. She moves back and her husband draws nearer.

"This is Devon," Sarah says.

"I am pleased to meet you, Father," I tell him, marveling at how much Sebastian looks like him, including the deep dimples now appearing on his cheeks as a smile spreads across his face.

He pulls me into his fatherly embrace and I feel like I am finally where I belong. Drawing back, he takes my face in his large hands.

"You are breathtaking!"

"Thank you."

He takes my arm, wrapping it around his. "Come. Your people await you."

Sebastian grins, taking his mother's arm, walking behind us.

"Now tell me, my dear," Devon says as we take the elevator down, "has my son been a gentleman through and through? He has a tendency to be naughty and a bit of a rebel from time to time."

Sarah clears her throat dramatically. "I think you have just described yourself, dear." Sebastian laughs at his father's feigned look of indignation.

"Nonsense, woman. I have never had a rebellious bone in my body."

Sebastian hoots out loud. "Now, Father, would you like me to tell Celine about the time you hid the city clock and–"

Devon clears his throat loudly. "We will have none of that," he says, his voice stern, then turns back to me. "Now where were we?"

Glancing at at Sarah's mirth-filled expression becomes too much and I cover my mouth, laughing out loud, the lovely woman quickly joining me. I finally wipe my eyes, meeting Devon's grinning expression. "He has been very much a gentleman," I finally say.

"Good, good! A chip off the old block, if I do say so myself."

Sarah releases an unlady-like snort and a fit of laughter hits us all. I again wipe my eyes, smiling at Sebastian.

I told you they would love you.

And I love them already. Devon grins down at me again. I am sure he felt my earlier anxiety and had taken it upon himself to help soothe my emotions. In that way, father and son really are alike.

When we reach the main floor, the elevator doors open and we are greeted by the city. The massive hall is full of grinning and cheering Challissians.

I'm in the land of giants! Sebastian's deep chuckle pierces the thought. The people make a path for us to walk through and I smile, returning the waves of the happy citizens as we make our way to the door. We exit and are greeted by even more cheers. It looks as if every citizen of Challis is here.

Devon presses my hand affectionately and I squeeze his back, grateful for such a warm welcome.

There is a hover car waiting for us at the curb. The sleek machine is black and looks like a cross between an Italian sports car and a limo, its metallic paint gleaming in the bright sunlight. Sebastian helps me into the back, his parents settling on the seat facing us. The driver loads our luggage into the trunk. Since the windows aren't tinted, I wave back at the people a moment before the car ascends into the air.

There are no words to describe the beauty of Challis. Though the photographs in the book were lovely, truly seeing this world with my own eyes is more amazing than I can say. I noticed as we walked through the crowd that there is no set style here as far as clothing. Some women wear updated fashions, some dress in Victorian era attire, which I love, and some even dress like pioneers. Though their dress is diverse, everyone is modest, and I decide I'm going to have to purchase some of the Victorian dresses. They will coordinate perfectly with my husband's standard but very attractive attire of silk white shirts, black leather pants and black boots. I quickly peruse his perfect form, drawing a sexy grin in return.

I'm pleased you appreciate the look and fit of my attire, beloved. And I assure you that the sight of you will forever warm my blood no matter what you choose to wear.

My cheeks immediately warm. Glancing at his parents, they give me a knowing grin in return.

Remember, you can close your thoughts to others, but your face speaks volumes.

Then I guess I should practice keeping my expression neutral.

"So, Father, what festivities are we in for this evening?"

"Well, a welcome celebration and performance has been planned for you in the amphitheater. Afterward, we will gather at the main hall for a big dinner provided by the citizens. Each family is contributing a dish, so there will be food galore."

"Yes," Sarah breaks in. "And a large amount of what is left over will go home with you. You won't need to cook for a week. Not that you really need to, anyway."

"That fact is still taking me some getting used to. Eating simply for pleasure and not because of need, plus, not having to worry about what or how much I eat is something most humans dream of."

"Are you truly happy with the changes, Celine?" she asks earnestly. "Are you really content with this new life?"

Meeting my husband's gaze, I smile. "I am happier and more content than I have ever been in my life. I will treasure the memories I have of my old life, but I wouldn't trade this one for anything. I only hope and pray that I can be worthy of the calling placed before me."

"Believe me, my dear," Devon says softly, "you are very worthy. *The One* chose you because of your worthiness. No one else can do what you will. No one else could be the mother of the golden child." He looks at his son. "And no one but our son could be your true mate. *The One* chose him long before he was born." He smiles. "Ours is a truly blessed family."

"Thank you." I am deeply humbled by their praise and their faith in us. With a heart full of gratitude, I turn and watch the passing scenery. The homes and buildings are beautiful and incredibly designed. Constructed of marbled granite and crystal, each one sparkles in the sun. Sebastian said his people lived in cottages, but to me, they look more like mini mansions.

We turn up a narrow, tree-lined path; it must be a mile long. At the end of the path sits an exquisite home. The granite and crystal building is topped with twelve tall spires connected by intricately carved arches. The huge double doors are white with gold trim. A granite fountain sits in the middle of a circular flower bed, and the large variety of flowers are all in full bloom. Of all the homes we've passed, this one is the most beautiful.

"Is this your home?" I ask Sarah.

"No, Celine. This is *your* home." She smiles at my flabbergasted expression.

Sebastian squeezes my hand. "You are the Woman of Prophecy, *cara*. This home was built especially for you."

When the vehicle stops, the driver gets out and unloads our luggage. Sarah loops her arm through mine as Sebastian and his father carry everything and we follow them in. We quickly explore each tastefully decorated room, and when we reach our room, Sarah helps me unpack. Opening the massive closet to hang some of my dresses, I notice a long white garment bag hanging in the corner. There is a black one as well.

"What is this?" I ask.

"This is your gown for tonight. The gathering is formal, so I picked one out for you, as well as a formal shirt and vest for Sebastian." Sarah unzips the bag and I suck in a breath as she reveals the regal gown. It is made of deep burgundy velvet, trimmed in gold silk with gold seed pearls around the scooped neck of the bodice. Crystal and gold pearls line the bottom, as well as the the long bell sleeves.

"It's exquisite," I say, thinking the word doesn't do the dress justice.

Sarah beams. "Somehow I knew you would love it. There are slippers to go with it," she adds, pointing to the dainty gold shoes on the shelf above the dress. "Sebastian's attire coordinates with your gown." She opens his bag, revealing a silky gold shirt with billowy sleeves, topped with a burgundy velvet vest trimmed in gold, accented with gold seed pearls. "You two will look stunning."

"I can't wait to wear it!"

"Sebastian will not be able to take his eyes off you–neither will the rest of the unbound men in attendance."

Blushing furiously, I lower my eyes. "I'm sure there will be plenty of single women there to keep them occupied."

"Well, let's hope so. Sebastian is so gifted at hearing the thoughts of others, no male within his range will leave with his inner organs intact." When my eyes widen she laughs softly. "I am only joking, dear. Well, maybe."

She winks. I love her sense of humor, as well as her husband's. Her joyful mood is contagious and I can't help feeling happy around her.

"May I ask you a question?"

She smiles. "You may ask me anything, dear."

"How do Challissians live so long? And how do you grow so tall?"

"Well, *The One* makes us immortal the moment we are conceived. And as for the height, part of it is genes, the other is the atmosphere in the earth's core. You know, a human weighing two hundred pounds on the surface would weigh only a hundred in Challis."

"Really? How is that possible?"

"You see, here in the earth's core we don't have the gravity issue. The body is lighter here. Everything is more buoyant."

"Wow," I whisper. I *had* noticed a difference when I stepped off the plane. "I know a few women who would love to loose weight with no effort. We could bottle Challissian air, sell it on the surface and make a fortune."

She laughs. "I will be sure to mention that to the city council."

"Just as long as you tell them the idea came from Sebastian."

"I will," she agrees, grinning. "Well, we should leave and give you two time to get settled in. We will return this evening to ride with you to the celebration."

"Thank you, Mother, for the dress, and for your acceptance of me."

She smiles, embracing me firmly. "Thank you for willingly accepting your calling, and for accepting our son. The love between bond mates is strong, but that which exist between you two is the strongest I have ever witnessed." She presses a gentle hand to my cheek. "And as for accepting you, anything else would be impossible. Besides," she adds with a smile, "you are very easy to love. You were meant to be a part of our family, and for this, we will be eternally grateful."

Blinking against the tears filling my eyes I thank her. She kisses my forehead and leaves in search of her husband. I follow her out, meeting Sebastian as he is seeing his father to the door. Devon embraces me, adding his own kiss to my cheek.

"Until this evening," he says, taking his wife's arm.

"Until this evening," Sebastian repeats, closing the door after them. He turns to me, drawing me to him. "How do you like your new home so far?"

"It's amazing!" I answer, wrapping my arms around his neck. "I never imagined it would be so incredible. There is so much diversity here, just like on the rest of the planet. Except I feel nothing but peace here. I felt the love of the people when we walked through the crowds. It's wonderful."

"They do love you. They have awaited the day that they could see you with their own eyes, to finally be in the presence of the Woman of Prophecy."

"I can't help feeling undeserving of the praise and ardor. I mean, it's the child who will fulfill the prophecy, not me."

"But you are the vessel, beloved. Without your willing and selfless heart there would be no golden child. Never forget how blessed you are. Never doubt your importance." Leaning down, he presses his forehead to mine, closing his eyes. "I am very blessed to have you," he whispers. "To be

117

chosen to share in this prophecy with you, to be given the priceless gift of your love, to be the recipient of your heart and have you own mine. I will be thankful for these blessings every single day of forever."

The tears that come now are unstoppable. He takes my face in his hands, kissing them away. With his loving words, the doubts and fears I have harbored inside slip away and are no more.

Twelve

Are you ready, beloved? Sebastian asks me as we prepare to enter the amphitheater. I can't answer him at the moment because I am so nervous, I can hardly breathe. It isn't fear now that incapacitates my tongue, but a desperate hope I carry inside that I look all right and will make my new family proud, doing nothing to bring shame to them. This is all so new for me–worrying about making a good impression, hoping people will think well of me–it's very disconcerting. Taking in my husband's regal attire, I marvel at how wonderful the gold shirt and burgundy vest look on him. He wears this with his standard black leather pants and I've decided leather pants must have been invented just for him because he wears them so well. His silky black hair is unbound, gently falling around his shoulders.

Sarah and Devon look amazing in their coordinating colors of forest green and gold. Sarah's long blond hair has been curled, the sides held back by two gold combs, curls flowing down her back. Devon's black hair is bound by a gold silk tie. The two make a very beautiful couple.

Finally glancing down at myself, I feel rather regal in my gown. I call the style "Victorian meets Renaissance," because both periods are blended into one, forming the perfect gown for me. My hair is pinned high on my head while a few curls fall against my face, the rest cascading down to the middle of my back. Because of the change in my skin and eyes, I only use a little makeup now, mainly mascara and eyeliner, which is a major time saver. Still, I hope I won't have makeup meltdown and don raccoon eyes before the end of the evening.

You are absolutely beautiful, beloved. There is no one more beautiful. And you will always make us proud.

Squeezing his hand, I kiss his cheek. He knows just what to say to calm my anxiousness and I never doubt his sincerity. Taking a deep breath, I give the three my best smile. "Okay," I say bravely, "let's do this." Devon and Sarah quickly cover their mouths, muffling a giggle and Sebastian grins, kissing my hand.

"All right, my lady," he says, amusement in his rich voice, "let's do this."

* * *

Sebastian's parents enter first and we follow. Startled, I suck in a breath when the entire crowd stands and applauds us as we descend the red-carpeted steps. Feeling Sebastian squeeze my hand gently, I lift my smiling eyes to his, completely comforted by the overwhelming love I feel radiating from the citizens of Challis. Little children stand with their parents, cheering with young voices as we make our way to the seats reserved for us in front, close to the stage. Before we sit, Sebastian and I turn to the crowd and wave for a moment, wanting the people to know we gratefully acknowledge their love.

When we are finally seated, a distinguished looking man come out on stage and welcomes us with a speech that touches our hearts. He shares the gratitude of the people for our arrival and pronounces a blessing upon our marriage–a blessing of hope and happiness. Then he pays a special tribute to Sebastian for diligently fulfilling his calling as my guardian, my protector, and my true mate, to which the crowd responds with thunderous applause. Sebastian's eyes meet mine, our love for one another shining through our mutual gaze.

Our host ends his remarks and the program begins.

Many citizens share their gifts and talents. A mother and daughter sing a song from a Challissian opera, each of them owning the voice of an angel. A young woman plays a piece on the flute while her brother accompanies her on the piano. A group of young girls perform a dance number from the surface world ballet, *Swan Lake,* and I am sure the piece was chosen just for me.

Two brothers perform a juggling act with balls, fruit, and . . . unless my eyes are deceiving me, cats? Hearing the loud meows, I cover my mouth, shocked. These peaceful people are juggling cats? Hysterical laughter rips through the audience. I turn to Sebastian and he bites his lip to keep from laughing at my expression, but soon gives up.

They are not real, beloved. They look it, but they aren't. The Olsen brothers have performed this act for centuries, always using stuffed animals. The meows are coming from back stage.

Oh. My relieved expression and the one word response has Sebastian shaking with laughter. *Well, I didn't know,* I say, finally joining him.

There are several more performances, some musical and some comical. Each one is done well and met by warm applause. At the end of the final performance, the host thanks everyone who performed, as well as the guest for attending. He then announces it is time to adjourn to the great hall for the welcome dinner. Everyone remains seated while we are escorted from the theater before standing to leave. Since the hall is only a block away, we walk.

On the way over, I express to Sebastian and his parents how much I enjoyed the program.

"I'm glad," Sarah says. "All the performers have been rehearsing for days and were deeply honored to be asked to participate."

"They were very talented and I enjoyed them all."

"Especially the cat juggling," Sebastian says. Grinning, I discreetly give him a playful shove before resting my hand on his on his arm. He laughs, placing his hand over mine.

Sorry, angel, but I just couldn't resist.

Squeezing his arm, I smile lovingly. *I know.*

* * *

The hall is festively decorated in bright colors, from the tablecloths to the fresh cut flowers that adorn each table, to the crystal and brass chandeliers draped in shimmering brightly-colored garland. There are four long tables set around the hall, each filled to capacity with delectable dishes of food.

Sliced roast beef, so tender it simply falls apart. Mini rotisserie chickens. Juicy slices of roasted pork. Buttery garlic potatoes. Vegetable kabobs. Salads made of tropical fruits. Fresh field greens tossed in a vinaigrette dressing. Luscious breads and pastries. Cakes and pies. The variety of food goes on and on. I almost wish I had a bigger plate to fit everything on. Instead, I pace myself by having just one taste of each thing. And every single dish I try is delicious.

We sit at a long table facing the guests. Many come up during the course of the meal to say hello and introduce themselves. When Sebastian and I are done eating, he links my arm through his and we wander around the hall, mingling. Some are shy and hesitant when we approach, and I understand the feeling well. I smile warmly, trying to make them feel at ease. The last thing I want is to be intimidating and have people afraid to talk to me. Every person I meet is kind and thoughtful, wishing us the best and promising to keep us in their prayers.

As the evening grows late, we thank everyone for their kindness and tell them of our appreciation for the wonderful welcome. And just as Sarah warned, we are sent home with a good amount of food, almost a week's worth.

Devon and Sarah have a hover car delivered and present it to us as a wedding gift, surprising us both. The sleek black vehicle is a smaller version of the one they picked us up in when we arrived. We thank them profusely and they send us off with loving embraces.

* * *

When we reach our home, we put the food away, each of us heaving a deep sigh as we come to the end of a very full day. Except for the memorable moments I spent with

Sebastian before coming here, I have never enjoyed myself more than today.

"Come out to the courtyard with me," he says, taking my hand.

"All right."

Hand in hand we walk through the softly-lit hallway, our bare feet quiet on the tile floor. We exit a set of beautifully-etched double glass doors; all the doorways are very tall, I notice. Stopping next to one of the white stone columns, Sebastian wraps his arms around me and I lean back against his solid chest as we gaze out at the enchanting landscape around us. The colors are vivid, our surroundings completely perfect.

"The skies are so beautiful here. This whole no darkness thing will take me some getting used to, but it is still beautiful."

He nods, chuckling softly. "Truthfully, the dark nights will be the one thing I'll miss about living on the surface. I missed it when we moved back from Italy as well. However, when I was younger, I discovered a way to bring the stargazing moments back with me."

"Oh, really?" I ask, intrigued. "What did you do?"

"Well, When I had just started my training, I would come home each night and lie out in the grassy field behind our home and stare up at the sky. Then I would close my eyes and envision the surface sky. After focusing really hard for a moment, the night sky was suddenly before me. The moon was always a crescent or half full and the stars were so bright."

"Wow! Would you teach me how to do that sometime?"

"I would be happy to." He pauses a moment, becoming thoughtful. "On those nights, I would lay for a while and wish with all my heart that when my calling as guardian to the Woman of Prophecy had ended, I would find my true mate. I used to dream she was somewhere in our world or on the surface, just waiting for me, and that that once I fulfilled my duty, the fates would lead us to each other."

"Really?" I love it when he shares cherished memories with me.

"Really," he says, resting his cheek against my hair. "Every night I wished for the same thing, never altering my wish in any way. Then something amazing happened."

"What happened?" I press when he pauses.

"On the night of my twenty-fifth birthday, my training session ended early. I celebrated with my parents, then went out to my usual spot. I lay out a little longer than normal, and again poured out my wishes for my true mate. I tried to imagine what she would look like. After a while I began to feel guilty for all the time I spent selfishly wishing for a mate when all my efforts should have been spent expressing gratitude for the honor of being a guardian. As soon as I replaced my selfish wishes with hope for the fulfilling of the prophecy, I saw a beautiful light trail across my envisioned sky. I was shocked! A shooting star had never been a part of my created night sky. As I watched it, I began to feel a warmth inside I had never felt before."

He tightens his embrace. "Each night after that, I went out and lay for the exact amount of time, and the light appeared at exactly the same moment, never altering in time. "I started calling it the wishing hour."

"The wishing hour," I softly repeat. "A fitting name." I smile, picturing him camped out on the grass, waiting to see the sight that had awed him so.

"I knew it was a sign from *The One*, telling me that all would be well." Pressing his lips against my ear, he softly says, "And he was right. He knew the path my life would take because He placed me on it. Being bound to you was my destiny."

I turn to him and gently pull his head down, meeting his lips with mine. "How grateful I an for that."

* * *

As Sebastian soaks in the warmth of his wife's embrace, he struggles to keep his thoughts and emotions free of everything except the intoxicating heat generating between them. Though he is happy to have succeeded in bringing her to the safety of his world, he knows the enemy isn't done and is just taking a brief pause. Lord Derth will work harder now. He will not stop until Celine is no longer a threat. Though the location of their home is hidden, they will still have to be on their guard more now than ever.

Pushing these thoughts away, he clings to her, vowing that the enemy will never get near her again.

* * *

An underground fortress near Mount St. Helens, Washington

A group of eight Urchin stand in the throne room before the being that is Lord Derth. To the world, he looks like any other man, but power corrupted and corroded his soul ages ago, leaving only the shell of a man.

He looks into the face of each creature he created–created for one purpose: to seek out and destroy the woman who would bear the golden child, or if possible, bring her to him so he will have the opportunity of looking in her eyes before killing her himself. The child must not be allowed to enter the world, for the very moment of its birth would be the evil lord's last. He and all those with him would be destroyed.

"What news of the search?" he asks the leader of the Urchin guard of assassins.

"We tracked them to northern Canada."

"And?" Lord Derth presses when the minion says nothing else.

"We lost them."

"And why are you here and not still out searching?"

"My lord, we lost all trace of them. The trail stops cold at Ellesmere Island. Beyond it there is nothing."

"Well, evidently they reversed their route and you missed them."

The Urchin continues to speak bravely. "That is impossible, my lord. We were posted all over Canada. If they had changed their direction we would have known. They would not have gotten past us."

Lord Derth rubs his bearded chin in contemplation. Currently he wears the facade of a medieval knight. His blond hair is slicked back from his forehead and he is dressed in full body armor, as if readying himself for battle.

"Surely you don't believe they could have just disappeared into thin air."

"We have no explanation, my lord, just that they traveled north."

Lord Derth again ponders silently. There is nothing more north than Ellesmere Island, nothing but snow and ice. Men travel to the North Pole frequently. Could their home be at the North Pole or somewhere near? It is a distinct possibility. He eyes the Urchin leader.

"Prepare your guard to make a thorough sweep of the North Pole. If there is no sign of them, then it is possible they changed course at the Pole and traveled to Russia or Greenland. Dismissed."

His eyes follow the group of Urchin as they exit. Lifting a gold chalice to his lips, he leans back in the large bejeweled gold chair.

"Where are they?" he questions aloud, again rubbing his chin. "Where indeed?"

Thirteen

"Very good. Try it again."

Standing by a small rosebush on the edge of the courtyard, I close my eyes and again open my mind. When I finally look again, the bush that had only donned a few unopened buds is now three times its size and is covered in brilliant red and white blooms.

"Excellent!" Sebastian praises. "You have learned to fully communicate with the land. Your heart truly knows the earth is a living, breathing entity and has a spirit. Instead of commanding the plant to grow, you openly asked and it complied." His smile is wide. "You are a natural, beloved."

I grin, admiring my handiwork, and marvel at how far I have come in my training, and how quickly I've been able to grasp everything.

For the past two months, my days have consisted of learning not only the laws and customs of Challis, but how to use my new abilities as well. In the mornings, Sebastian attends meetings at the town hall with his father, where they discuss the welfare of the people. Afterward, he spends two hours training new warriors. For the duration of the day, he devotes every spare moment to helping me master myself in both mind and body. He has been a very patient teacher, and thanks to his diligence, I can move objects, change their structure, fight and defend myself should I need to (very important to me, since learning that other than receiving a fatal blow to the heart, the only thing that can kill us would be the loss of a mate, because neither can survive without the other) and read the thoughts of others. But my favorite feat is dressing and undressing with no effort. Sebastian favors that ability as well.

"That is enough for today," he says, walking towards me, pride showing in his eyes. He pulls me close. "How does a run out to the country sound? Give us an opportunity to stretch our legs."

"It sounds wonderful," I say, kissing him. "But we need to be back in time to go to your parent's place for dinner."

"I think we can accomplish that. I am ready when you are."

Glancing down at my skinny jeans, peach tunic, and black Mary Jane walking shoes, I decide it is the perfect outfit for this most enjoyable activity. I zoom upstairs and grab a blanket, back at his side before he can blink. When I grin he laughs. "I'm ready."

I love the feeling of exhilaration I get when we run, and the freedom is indescribable. I've never really considered running fun before, just a lot of hard and exhaustive work. But I definitely don't feel that way anymore.

* * *

Twenty minutes later, I am sitting on a blanket in the middle of a lush, green grassy field. Sebastian's eyes are closed, his head resting in my lap. Softly running my fingers through his silky mane, I take in the scenery as we soak in the peace surrounding us. Using my fine-tuned senses, I inhale the intoxicating fragrances of flowers, pine trees, and grass laced with the subtle scent of wildlife and fresh water from the four massive waterfalls running down the sides of the distant mountains. Across the large field, a family of leopards lounge in the sun. I smile, watching the mother grooming her little cub. In a nearby tree, a band of Kampuchea monkeys sit on the limbs, chattering away. On a far hill, a herd of sheep graze peacefully. Beyond my view, I sense the presence of mammoths, large elk, kangaroos, various other animals, and even several types of dinosaurs.

It is still hard for me to believe they exists here, even though I've walked among the peaceful creatures several times since arriving. All the animals live together in harmony, and it goes without saying that Challis is a place unlike any other.

"Do you think we will ever let the outside world know Challis exists?" I ask.

"I don't know. Maybe someday. If *The One* wills it."

I contemplate his answer. "Do you think it would be possible for anyone to find this place?"

"I pray not. We do everything in our power to keep that from happening. The warriors on the surface are especially careful when they return." He pauses a moment. "Now that you are here, things will most likely change. No one else will be leaving and the few that live on the surface are being called home. We have always done what we could to help the people without interfering, but the outer world becomes more corrupt every day and there is only so much we have been allowed to do. The natural man isn't as strong as he once was and the enemy preys on their weaknesses. And though Lord Derth's minions are not allowed to be seen, some humans make it easy for their bodies to be used by the Urchins. Now the people must be left on their own while we prepare."

He finally opens his eyes and smiles. "Hopefully, one day soon you will conceive. With pregnancy only lasting five months, peace is just around the corner."

Caressing his face, heated by the warmth of his gaze, I decide it is time. Fully opening my thoughts to him, I allow what I have hidden for the past week to move to the forefront of my mind, having held back only because I needed to be sure. His blue eyes widen and he immediately sits up, staring at me. His sensuous mouth opening slightly, he gently takes my face in his hands.

"You are with child?" he asks in wonder, as if he needs verification by hearing me speak the words.

"Yes," I answer with tears in my voice, as well as my eyes. "Another part of the prophecy is being fulfilled, my love."

He laughs and I feel the magnitude of his joy welling up inside me. Pulling me close, he kisses me deeply, and I melt against him as words of love spill from his thoughts into mine, heating the very core of me.

You are my heart, beloved. My heart and my soul.

"And you are mine," I whisper against his lips.

He draws back slightly, caressing my face with his gaze. "We must tell Mother and Father, and then the council."

I nod, suddenly guarding my thoughts. The immediacy in which I shut him out hits him hard and he grunts softly.

"What is it?" His voice and eyes are filled with concern. "What's wrong?"

"I'm scared."

"Why are you afraid?" As I slowly open my thoughts to him again, he understands. "You again feel unworthy of the calling and wonder if you will be a good enough mother."

I nod, disappointed that hearing my concerns voiced out loud does not make me feel at least a little relieved. "He will need to be taught so much, not only about life, but about his people, his destiny. Not to mention I don't know the first thing about babies or raising a child."

Sebastian smiles, caressing my face, resting his warm hand on the back of my neck beneath my hair. "You will be a wonderful mother, Celine. I think it will be as natural to you as breathing. And as for your worthiness, *The One* chose you *because* he deemed you worthy." Caressing my neck, he buries his hands in my hair and presses his forehead to mine. "*The One* does not make mistakes, beloved."

Releasing a deep breath, I let his comments settle. I have always felt *The One's* presence, but since arriving in Challis, I've felt it a great deal more. It always leaves me with a sense of peace. I draw upon that peace now. Touching his face, I slowly trail a finger across his lips. "You will be a wonderful father."

Saying nothing else, he simply presses his mouth to mine, and the last traces of my concern fade into nothingness.

Fourteen

The Challissian council consists of the president, twelve counselors, and one hundred forty-four thousand peace keepers. The council meets every afternoon in a large room on the upper floor of the town hall. A beautiful edifice, the crystal and white granite building coordinates with the rest of the elegant structures. It houses fifteen floors of offices and boasts a large glass clock above the top floor. Thinking about the clock reminds me of Sebastian's remark about his father hiding it, which Devon hastily interrupted. I make a mental note to bring it up again later.

As we share our news with the council, the same love radiates from them that I felt from Sebastian's parents when we told them of my pregnancy before coming here.

President Simon approaches me and takes my hand.

"We are so happy for you, for our people, and for the world above. For peace is coming soon. In your womb lives our future."

Swallowing hard, I nod, smiling at the older man, and study his kind features. A foot shorter than Sebastian, President Simon looks down at me through wise, green eyes that have seen much in life. His long blond hair is pulled back and secured with a gray leather thong, the color of which matches his tunic. Like the rest of the Challissian race, his features are perfect. I momentarily wonder if our child will be as perfect since I was once mortal, then quickly put the thought out of my mind. Sebastian's blood now flows through my veins and I am one of his people now. Nothing else matters.

"Tonight we will announce this joyful news to the people, that all prayers might be with you."

"Thank you," I say and he bows.

Taking my hand, Sebastian leads me from the office, his parents following us. When we are outside the building, Devon and Sarah embrace me.

"How are you feeling?" she asks.

"I feel wonderful!" I grin jubilantly and they laugh. "I don't feel like they say you're supposed to feel when you're pregnant, but I guess that is to be expected."

"Indeed," Sarah says. "In another week or so, your stomach will start expanding quickly. So quickly in fact, you will need a new wardrobe weekly." She laughs at my look of dismay. "Roomy tunics and elastic waist trousers will work nicely, but you will need to have gowns made that can adjust to accommodate growth. Tomorrow I will take you to my friend Rachael's shop. She will make sure you have everything you need."

"Sounds good. I definitely enjoy shopping."

Sebastian laughs, pulling me close. "Clothes are her hobby, Mother. You two are kindred spirits."

"Yes," Devon says. "Remind Mother to give you a tour of her closet sometime. The woman has an surface earth shopping mall in there."

Sarah shoots her husband an exasperated frown. "Women need variety. It's not just for us, you know. We do it for you men."

"Of course you do, dear. And we are very appreciative of that fact." He pulls her close, bringing a soft smile to her face and a twinkle to her bright eyes. "We count ourselves fortunate men to be the property of the two most beautiful women on or in the planet."

"Amen," Sebastian agrees.

* * *

A gentle breeze from the ceiling fan stirs the sheer curtains hanging in our bedroom window. With all the window panes in the house darkened to shield the daylight, I lay in our massive bed on my back and stare up at the expansive night sky on our ceiling. With our combined efforts, we draw on memories of the night sky on the surface and recreate the visual above us. The stars twinkle brightly and the half moon displays its beautifully-shadowed craters. In our night sky, Saturn, Jupiter, Venus, and Mars loom in the distance. It is a most perfect vision and an amazing display.

The silky white sheets are comfortable and cool against my skin, and because we can't hear the real thing through closed windows, the replicated sounds of chirping crickets and croaking frogs serenade us with a soft night symphony. A few fireflies hover just inside the window, their florescent lights blinking on and off, creating a separate light show.

A feeling of contentment washes over me as Sebastian caresses my bare, still-flat stomach. He lightly rests his head on me with his ear pressed against my skin. Not an hour ago, I felt movement for the first time. I couldn't believe it! It had been light, but I could definitely feel it. Now we lay peacefully, communing with our son.

"You know," I finally say, "I have to remind myself that even though his birth will change the world, he will still be just a baby, with the same needs of any other baby. He will need us to love and care for him, teach him to walk, to talk, to be obedient, and to love *The One* above all things." I sigh. "It is a bit overwhelming to think about."

He softly kisses my stomach. "As I said before, I am sure motherhood will be as natural to you as breathing. Our son could not be blessed with a better mother."

"Nor a better father," I say, burying my fingers in his hair. It seems we cannot be near one another without touching in some way. It is impossible. However, we treasure moments like these, being wrapped up in one another. And though we will have a little one soon, these moments will never cease. We will make sure of that.

"Do you think he will know–when he's older–of the importance of his birth? Will we need to tell him, or will we raise him as a normal child?"

He adjusts his head to look at me. "I think something inside him will know what the purpose is for his life. We must teach him his history, why his birth was so anticipated. But he must understand that his life will also be an example, and the way he lives it will touch all those he comes in contact with. With *The One's* help, we will teach him to cultivate unconditional love, to be a true friend, to be honest, and to treat others the way he would want to be treated." He smiles, touching my face. "He will grow into a good man one day."

"Like his father," I say.

"He will be much better than me." Settling himself next to me, he takes me in his arms, sighing as he whispers against my temple his final thought of the night. "I can ask no more than that."

Fifteen

Standing only half a foot taller than me, with flaming red hair and sea green eyes, dressed in a belted, bright fuchsia, floral ankle-length dress, Rachael Walton is a breath of fresh air with an underlying tornado attached. She is bold, beautiful and bubbly, with a major flair for fashion, and I can see why expectant mothers flock to her shop. Every article of clothing she designs is a masterpiece and no two pieces of clothing are the same. Shopping at Rachael's means knowing you are getting the best quality for a more than fair price. Not to mention she is a joy to be around. I can definitely understand why she and Sarah are such good friends.

Knowing what I do about her personal life, I am impressed with her effervescent personality, her wit and charm. Before coming to Rachael's shop, Sarah shared a little about her friend with me. Having lost her husband in battle with the enemy on the surface, she has been alone for over a hundred years, which I find amazing. Her mate bravely gave his life while protecting my ancestors so my bloodline would continue and I could be born. Because of this, I felt an immediate kinship with the woman, as well as a great sense of gratitude for her sacrifice. Her parents have been living on the surface for the past fifty years but have recently returned. She had missed them and is glad they are back.

In between indulging in peppermint tea and mini cream puffs, I try on colorful feminine tunics, coordinating elastic-waist slacks, and adjustable-waist gowns, as well as one-of-a-kind sandals and slippers. I instantly fall in love with each outfit I try and purchase them all.

"You are a very talented lady, Rachael," I say as she folds my purchases and places them in four large shopping bags.

"Well, thank you, dear, but *you* make the outfits beautiful."

I smile, blushing slightly. "Thank you. I'm looking forward to wearing your masterpieces."

"And I am looking forward to hearing of your husband's reaction once he sees you in them." She leans close and whispers conspiratorially, yet loud enough for

Sarah to hear, "Between you and me, he won't be able to keep his hands off you."

Sarah chuckles. "He already can't do that!"

The two women laugh and I join them, still blushing furiously. Sarah and I each take two bags. "Thank you again," I say to Rachael as she walks us to the door.

"You're very welcome. Come back and see me soon."

"I will."

* * *

Sebastian enters the closet just as I finish putting everything away, and he peruses my new wardrobe. "I'm looking forward to seeing you in these."

"Well, you won't have long to wait. Rachael told me you won't be able to keep your hands off me when you see me in these outfits, and your mother assured her that you can't keep them off off me now."

Sebastian's eyes widen and he laughs. "That's Mother for you. She speaks her mind." He pulls me close. "But she is always truthful."

"I'm surprised she didn't include me as well. It's pretty hard for *me* to keep my hands off *you*."

"And for that I am grateful."He laughs, kissing my neck. "It's all my father's fault. I take after him."

"I can believe that. And speaking of your father, what's the story with him hiding the town clock?"

"My father will have my head for this," he says with a sly smile. "But since you are family, you are entitled to know his deep dark secret."

"Do tell."

We make ourselves comfortable on the leather sofa in the sitting area of our room. "Well, it all started with his friend, Saul. Saul is in charge of maintenance at the town hall, which includes the clock. One day the clock stopped working. My father mentioned it to Saul, and he in turn told Father that he would get around to repairing it sometime.

* * *

"Sometime!" Devon replied in shock. "What do you mean sometime? It needs to be repaired now. The President requires order in the kingdom, and a broken city clock is definitely not considered order."

"Well, it's not like our lives depend on the thing," Saul said. "Everyone has a clock or two in their homes. What difference does it make if the town clock isn't working? Life will still go on, my friend, working clock or no."

Devon said nothing else, just bid his friend goodbye and left. A week later the clock still hadn't been repaired, so Devon decided to teach Saul a lesson. Late that night after making sure no one was around to see his dastardly deed, he took the clock down, brought it home, and stored it in one of the guest rooms. Since he had been ranting to his wife and son about the non-working clock non-stop, the two watched him hide it while mumbling to himself about work ethic and clock neglect, and fell against each other laughing.

"The next day, Devon watched from a distance as Saul walked toward the building entrance, looked up, and froze as he gazed at the spot where the clock had been. The man released a frantic shriek and hurried into the building. Devon entered the town hall a minute after Saul and caught up with him in the elevator, slipping in just before the doors closed.

"Good morning, my friend, he greeted. How are you today?"

"Did you see?! The clock is gone!"

"Oh, how terrible!"

"I can't believe it. Who would do something so underhanded?"

"I could not venture to guess," Devon said, suppressing a smile.

"I just don't understand," Saul said, scratching his head in puzzlement. "I mean who . . ." He paused and looked at his friend, his eyes narrowing suspiciously. "It was you, wasn't it? I know it was you!"

"I have no idea what you're talking about. What would I want with a large defective clock?"

"You did it to get back at me, didn't you?"

"I have never been one for revenge, and I'm appalled that you could think that of me."

148

"What did you do with it?" Saul's voice was suddenly pleading. "You must tell me what you've done with it. I can tell the President that I took it home to make the repairs and plan to bring it back as soon as I have finished."

"But you haven't been working on it. You had not even planned to work on it."

"Please," Saul pleaded, beads of sweat appearing on his forehead. "I promise I will prepare it today. Just tell me where it is."

"Do I have your word?"

"Yes! Just tell me where it is."

Devon smiled. "Go home and check your living room."

"Go home? What do you mean go home? I don't have it!"

"You do now."

* * *

"It seems Father had visited with Saul's wife two days before and told her of his plan. Because she knew what a procrastinator her husband was, she happily agreed to assist Father in his scheme. When Saul finally got home, he was greeted with the vision of the clock topped with a big pink bow. He immediately made the repairs and took the clock back. And he never procrastinated repairs again."

I roar with laughter, picturing the whole incident. I can see Devon doing it all–hauling the clock away and hiding it, then waiting for Saul to leave for work before taking it and placing it in his friend's living room."

"That is just too priceless," I say, wiping my eyes. "Your father is a riot."

"He's something," Sebastian says, causing us both to start laughing all over again. When he finally stops, he says, "Please make sure I'm not around when you bring the story up with Father. His eyes will shoot fire darts through me and I will be maimed for eternity."

"Don't worry," I say, still laughing. "I will keep you safe. You have my word."

Sixteen

Standing in front of a full length mirror with Sebastian's arms wrapped around me, his large hands on my bare abdomen, we gaze at the reflection of my growing round stomach. Sarah had been right. I did start to show a week after our announcement, and now, a month later, my midsection has doubled in size. I am halfway through my pregnancy and I feel wonderful. Our son is extremely active, his kicks and movements growing stronger with each passing day.

"I think I want to stay home and be lazy with you today," Sebastian says, burying his face in my hair.

"That sounds good to me," I murmur, closing my eyes. "However, the council will be awaiting your arrival. I don't think they would call wanting to be lazy with your wife a good excuse for not attending a meeting."

"True, but it *is* a good excuse to *me*." His longing eyes meet mine in the mirror. "I'm going to let my assistant handle the training class today. I will return to you after my workout."

I kiss him. "And I will be waiting," I murmur against his mouth." I walk him to the door and he embraces me once more before reluctantly releasing me. "I love you."

"And I love you." Kissing me another long moment, he finally pulls away.

I shut the door and head back upstairs to shower. After dressing, I make the bed, dedicate a few moments to commune with *The One*, eat, tidy the already clean house, then pull out my straw crocheting tote and head to the garden room, stopping by the kitchen on the way. Making myself comfortable on the sofa, I place a cup of herbal tea on the square glass table beside me. I absolutely adore this room. It is completely enclosed in floor-to-ceiling beveled glass windows. A large white area rug covers the middle of the gray tile floor and there are both hanging and standing plants in each corner. The two over-size green and ivory striped chairs with matching ottomans coordinate with the sofa and all the glass tables are topped with white and gray tatted lace. A panel on the wall next to the double French doors and a remote on the table control the windows, tinting them when the sun is too bright, and adjusting the shades which lower from the ceiling to give the room total privacy. An electronic picture frame sits on the table next to me, displaying alternating images of Sebastian and I and his parents. This is my favorite room in the house, coming in second only to our bedroom.

Opening the basket, I take out the baby afghan I have been working. The light blue yarn is the softest I have ever felt. I had purchased several pastel colors two weeks ago and have finished six afghans so far. Yellow, green, purple, lavender, white, and turquoise ones now sit folded on a shelf in the nursery upstairs, along with a chest full of baby clothes.

I could make a hundred of these in a couple of hours, but I prefer going slower because it's so relaxing. My mother taught me to crochet when I was ten and I've kept it up through the years, crocheting blankets to give as gifts. Once I started working at the rest home, I began crocheting afghans and donating them for the residents there.

Thinking of my elderly friends, which I do occasionally, I wonder how they are. I also think of Karen and Sarah, and hope Karen took Sebastian's counsel and left her abusive husband. I miss my friends and wish I could see them again.

But I wouldn't trade my life now for anything. Besides, I'm sure there will be a chance to see them again one day.

Changing the course of my thoughts, I let them drift to my husband. Every single day, every single moment I spend with him is blissful. I never imagined that marriage could be so wonderful. Sebastian is perfect for me in every way. Of course, he would have to be, to be my true mate. There are no secrets between us, and our minds, hearts, and souls lay completely open to each other. There is nothing I can't tell him or he can't tell me. I am literally the blood of his blood, bone of his bone, and flesh of his flesh. I feel him moving inside my soul and I in his. We are one in all things. No outer earth couple could ever be so deeply connected. I mean, a married couple can feel deep love for one another, sure, but here in Challis, it goes so beyond that. Here, the love shared between a true-mated husband and wife is everything. It is the essence of all we are. If *The One* had not chosen me to be the Woman of Prophecy, to be Sebastian's true mate, and I had married someone on the surface, I'm sure I would have loved him very much, raised a family, and enjoyed a happy life, but there could never have been the connection I feel with Sebastian. I would never have known such rapture, such openness, such oneness with another soul.

Feeling a sudden warmth, I close my eyes as Sebastian's voice travels over the distance between us and enters my mind.

I adore you as well, beloved. You are on my mind always.

Am I disturbing you? I ask him.

Never.

When we are apart I miss you.

I miss you as well.

I'm still amazed that a part of me can be with you, that I can still talk to you, feel you when you're not here.

It never grows old, does it?

It never will. I am counting the hours until you are home.

I am as well. But until then, imagine my arms around you, my mouth pressed against yours, my voice whispering words of love in your ear. Can you feel me? Can you taste my kiss? Can you hear me?

A warm shudder comes over me, runs through me. *I feel you, my love. I taste your kiss, and I hear your voice whispering to me. Thank you. I will be fine now until you are here.*

His voice is no longer here, but I still feel the warmth of him wrapped around me like an embrace. I sigh and continue crocheting the afghan, finishing it faster than I had planned. *Oh, well.* I put the hook and unused yarn back into the tote and fold the afghan, pressing it against my cheek a moment, enjoying the softness. I am about to head upstairs when the doorbell rings. I place the basket and blanket on a table in the hallway.

Opening the door, I am pleasantly greeted by a young man holding a large gift basket of fruit.

"I was asked to deliver this to you, my lady."

"Thank you," I say taking the basket. I open the card attached. Written in beautiful handwriting is the inscription, ***Best wishes to you, my lady. Health to you and your little one.***

"There is no signature. Do you know who sent it?"

"No, my lady. I was only told to bring it to you." He smiles. "Maybe the sender wanted it to be a surprise."

"Well, it definitely is," I say. "Thank you very much."

"You're most welcome," he says and quickly jogs back to his hover car.

I close the door and take the basket to the kitchen, placing it on the counter. Taking a ripe pear from the basket, I wonder if it is from Devon and Sarah. They know how much I love fruit, especially pears, and there seems to be more of them in the basket than anything else. I immediately bite into it and close my eyes, smiling as the juicy flavor bursts in my mouth.

Ahhh, I love eating for pleasure. Whoever sent the basket was very thoughtful. I have yet to meet an unkind person in Challis and I am grateful to be raising our child in a place with so much love. That's not to say he will never know unkindness, but he *will* know kindness first.

As I raise the pear to take another bite, nausea slowly creeps into me, a feeling I haven't experienced during my pregnancy so far. Placing the pear on the table, I close my eyes, swallowing against the sick feeling, but it only grows worse. Taking a deep breath, I wipe the beads of perspiration from my forehead. Unable to sit up any longer, I lean forward and rest my head against the table, wondering what is wrong with me. I'm not supposed to be able to get sick anymore, or at least normal Challissian women aren't.

I decide to lie down for a bit and see if that helps, but just as I stand up, a sharp pain shoots through me, starting in my stomach. The intensity causes me to double over. Then the sensation moves to my head. I tell myself that if I can make it to the bedroom to lie down I'll be okay. The pain increases, blinding me with force, and I stagger a few feet before collapsing on the floor.

Sebastian . . . help me . . . please. I say no more as everything goes dark.

Seventeen

As the pain seizes his mate, a thunderous roar escapes Sebastian, startling the counselors and rattling the windows of the conference room.

Celine!

Devon quickly moves to him. "What is it, son?"

Celine, can you hear me? When there is no answer, he says, "It's Celine. Something is wrong!"

As if they were one body, the president and his counselors immediately stand. Sebastian bolts from the room with his father and the rest of the men following him.

Hold on, beloved! he tells her. *Just hold on, I am coming!*

* * *

Making it home in record time, the front doors fly open with a wave of Sebastian's hands. "Celine!" he calls running to the kitchen, having sensed her location before he'd even entered the house. He finds her lying on the floor, her clothes drenched with sweat. He lifts her and races up the stairs past the group of men, yelling to his father, "Call the healer!"

Sebastian places his wife on the bed, then waves his hand over her, exchanging her wet clothes for a lightweight white chemise. He lifts her and pulls back the covers, drawing only the sheet over her. Running to the bathroom, he wets a wash cloth, then sits on the bed and gently presses the cool cloth against her forehead, dabbing the perspiration from her cheeks.

I am here, beloved, he mentally croons. *I am here.* He lifts her hand to his lips, holding it there. *Help is on the way, angel. All will be well.* He leans down, lightly resting his ear against her stomach. "Be well," he whispers to their child. "Your mother and I love you and we need you. All your people need you." He raises up and again presses the cloth against her forehead and cheeks. Never in his entire existence has he seen a face more beautiful, or felt a more beautiful soul. Earlier, he had felt the strength of her love wash over him, and it had caught him so off guard, he had been overwhelmed and could barely concentrate on the meeting. He remembers the smile President Simon shot him from across the table. He knew the older man couldn't read his mind, but he was sure his expression spoke volumes. He'd spent the remaining time anticipating being with his wife again. When the pain hit Celine, the force of it had staggered him more than a blow in battle ever had. The rage the sensation produced had even frightened *him*.

A moment later the healer enters the room. The silver-haired woman gives him a kindly smile, but he reads the worry in her deep-set eyes and her furrowed brow.

"Has she awakened at all?"

Sebastian tugs a hand back through his hair. "No, she hasn't." He watches the woman press a hand to Celine's forehead.

Frowning, the healer sits on the side of the bed, presses her hand against Celine's stomach, and closes her eyes.

"She has been poisoned," she says softly.

It takes every ounce of strength Sebastian possesses to stay seated and remain quiet. He feels like he will explode. Who dared hurt his mate? Who dared harm their child? When he finds out, absolutely nothing will stop him from destroying the enemy, for the person is indeed his enemy now.

"The poison is a bad one," she continues. "One I have never seen before." She slowly moves her hands over Celine's stomach and the rest of her body. "It isn't plant-based, so it must have come from the surface."

"The baby?" he questions.

Lightly resting her ear against Celine's stomach, the healer is quiet for another moment. She finally lifts her eyes and smiles. "Your son is healthy and strong. By some great miracle, his is unaffected."

"Good," he breathes. "And my wife?"

She finishes her examination. "Her body is beginning to fight off the poison. She will regenerate slowly. She will be sick and weak for a few days and drained of strength, but she will recover."

Sebastian heaves of deep sigh of relief and silently thanks *The One* for the gift of Celine's life. There would be no way he could survive without her. She is the life force that sustains him, the very marrow of his bones.

"During pregnancy is when our women are the most vulnerable. Not that we are weaker, but we have more than ourselves to be concerned about." She pauses, studying Celine a moment. "Stay by her side. If by some chance her condition should worsen, send for me at once."

He nods and takes the woman's hand, squeezing it firmly. "I will. And thank you."

* * *

Downstairs, before leaving, the healer gives Devon, President Simon, and his counselors the details of Celine's condition. After sharing their feeling of relief, warriors are summoned to the Giovanni's home and posted all around the house. They are instructed to admit no one into the house except Sebastian's parents, nor should gifts of any kind be accepted. There will be an immediate investigation. Celine and her unborn child are officially in danger now and every precaution possible will now be taken to insure their safety.

* * *

Once everyone has gone, Sebastian quietly undresses and slips between the sheets. Gathering his sleeping wife in his arms, he holds her close. He desperately needs to feels the warmth of her body against him, feel her deep breaths fanning him, and the beat of her heart next to his. The combination of those things gives him great comfort.

He will no longer attend meetings, nor will he conduct training sessions. Until the birth of their son, he will never leaver her side. He'd desired to spend more time with her and now he will have that time, he only wishes the circumstances were different. The thought of her being in danger causes him intense pain, and the last thing he ever expected was to have a traitor living in Challis. This is his home, a place that has existed in peace for thousands of years. A place where all who dwell here are safe. How can they have an enemy living among them and not notice? Whoever it is blends in pretty well and will be hard to find, but Sebastian is determined that the traitor will be found and made to pay for his crime.

Closing his eyes, he tightens his embrace and silently prays that Celine will soon awaken. He can do nothing else.

Eighteen

Awakening to darkness, the warmth of Sebastian's body is wrapped around me like a cocoon of safety. I am no longer in pain, but I am so weak, I can't even lift my head off the pillow.

What happened to me? The last thing I remember is feeling the awful pain explode in my head and stomach. I have never in my life experienced such pain. Fearing for our child, my hand immediately moves to my stomach.

"He is well, beloved," Sebastian softly assures me. "He is strong, and so are you."

"What happened to me?" I ask him, my voice hoarse.

He waves the lamp on and adjust himself to look into my eyes, though he doesn't release me, for which I am grateful. I need his closeness more now than ever.

"You were poisoned, *cara*."

I swallow hard. "Poisoned? But how?"

He gently cups my face and I see the pain in his eyes, hear it in his voice, though it is also laced with anger. "The fruit. It was injected with poison." Now there are tears in his eyes. "Someone tried to kill you and our child."

I am shocked beyond words. Someone tried to kill me! Tried to kill our son, the golden child! How could this happen in Challis? There is no evil here, only love, or at least there wasn't until now. And how could the poison affect me?

"It was a strong poison created on the surface. Strong enough to make you very sick, but your body was able to fight it off. You will be weak for a short time, but you will heal completely." He pauses and I lift a hand to his face, his warm tears wetting my fingertips. "I was so afraid I would lose you, Celine. I've never been so afraid in my life."

Pulling his head down, I press my face to his, our tears mingling. "You will never lose me, Sebastian. There is something inside me that will never let me be separated from you."

As he covers my mouth with his, my insides explode with heat. I'm amazed that even in sickness, his kiss can have this effect on me.

I love you, cara. *I love you so much. And I'm so sorry I wasn't here to keep you safe.*

You couldn't have known. And I love you, too.

Releasing my lips, he buries his face in my hair, pulling me further into himself, lulling me to sleep with the sound of his voice in my mind, whispering the same endearing phrase over and over.

I love you, my angel. I love you . . .

* * *

When I wake up the next morning, Sebastian's side of the bed empty. He enters the room a minute later with a pastry and a glass of juice, which I consume quickly, anxious to get on with the day. I can't do much, but I don't want to stay in bed all day, either.

After helping me bathe, dress, and tame my hair, Sebastian carries me down to the garden room, where to my surprise, my in-laws are waiting to see me. He places me on the sofa and sits next to me, placing my legs over his lap.

"Oh, my dear," Sarah says, drying her eyes and kneeling to embrace me, "I'm so glad you are all right and the baby is well."

"Thank you. I'm so glad you came to see me."

"A pack of wild mammoths couldn't keep us away," Devon says, kneeling, pulling me into his fatherly embrace. He draws back and grins, and I can't help laughing, which is what he'd hoped for.

"Any news?" Sebastian asks his father as he and Sarah pull the two ottomans close and settle themselves for our visit.

"None," Devon answers. "Peace keepers were immediately sent to the produce merchant to question the owner. There was never an order placed, and he'd had so many customers throughout the day, he couldn't possibly tell them who bought the fruit. However, he did say the pears were not from his stand. Evidently, they were from a private orchard."

Sebastian's thoughts are painfully open to me. His hand forms a fist, and when I cover it with mine, it loosens slightly.

"We won't stop searching," Devon continues. "All our warriors are home now, except for the few living above, keeping watch around the north and south openings to warn us of possible intruders. Sadly, none of our mortal helpers from the surface will be admitted into Challis. This had once been a possibility should their lives be in danger, but not anymore. We have been in contact with them and they all understand why we are taking this precaution." He puts his arm around Sarah and she tearfully squeezes my free hand. "No matter what, we will keep you safe. No more attempts will be made on your life because the traitor will never have another chance."

167

Nineteen

Devon and Sarah soon kiss me goodbye and Sebastian walks them to the door. Relaxing against the pillow, I stare out the window and listen to their soft voices echoing back to me from down the hall. Devon is again assuring Sebastian that they will not stop until the attempted murderer is found and admonishing him to take good care of me, the latter statement completely unnecessary, of course.

Through the open window, I hear birds chirping in the trees just beyond the courtyard. A hummingbird flutters near, landing on the feeder hanging just outside the window. I watch it as it drinks the sweet nectar and suddenly long to run out into the countryside again, but even if my life were not in danger, I wouldn't have strength enough to even walk half a mile. For a moment, a small vein of frustration seeps into me. I had thought when I came to live in Challis, my days of running and needing protection were over. Now it seems that once again my life is no longer in my control. The frustration quickly turns to sadness. It hurts to think of someone hating me enough to want me dead. But then again, I guess it is really our child they wish to destroy, which is even worse.

I absently press a hand over my stomach, feeling his gentle nudging in response to my touch. I love this child more than words can express, more than my own life, and if I have to sacrifice my life in some way to bring him safely into a world that desperately needs him, then so be it. I know Sebastian could not survive without me and his life would be forfeit as well, but I have no doubt that we are of one mind when it comes to the safety and protection of the golden child. His life and well being mean more than either of us. Closing my eyes against the tears threatening, I force them back. I will not cry now. I can't because if I start, I am not sure I will be able to stop. Against my will, they begin to seep through anyway. Just as the first warm tears trail down my cheeks, Sebastian returns. He sits down and immediately scoops me into his arms, holding me on his lap. The restraint I've manged to hold onto slips away and deep sobs escape me. I cling to him, soaking the front of his shirt, finding comfort in his tightened embrace and soft words.

* * *

I am here, beloved, he croons. *I am here.*

Sebastian felt her pain as soon as it came and had had to cut his goodbye with his parents short because of his mate's emotional need for him. He holds her as deep sobs wrack her body, feeling each one intimately. This is not the life he'd planned for her, yet this is what they have. What will come next, only *The One* knows. Still, deep inside, he knows all will be well in the end. These are the feelings he sends to her now, to calm and comfort her.

The One *is with us, beloved. He knows what we are going through, and we will not be left alone. There is a purpose to all life, my angel. The purpose of our life has been fixed since the beginning, and you and I are gifted to know exactly what our purpose is: to fulfill the prophecy. And it will be fulfilled. I promise you,* cara, *it will be fulfilled.*

Twenty

A week has passed and my health is completely restored. I feel well–so well in fact, I invite Sarah and Rachael over for tea and cakes and we have a wonderful visit. These two women could take the saddest, most down person in the world and within a minute or two have them smiling and forgetting about their troubles.

Rachael even created for me what she calls her "cheer up" dress. It is is made of the softest yellow crushed velvet with a scooped neck and long bell sleeves. The material is stretchy and hugs my curves, accentuating my growing abdomen. From the waist, the slim fit flares out and hangs to the top of my feet. The neck, sleeves and bottom are trimmed with small crystal beads. It is absolutely beautiful, and as soon as she presented it to me I put it on, leaving my feet bare. I feel more beautiful just wearing it, and definitely more cheered up. I thank her again for her thoughtfulness.

"Oh, you're very welcome," she says in her cheery, high-pitched voice. "It was no trouble at all and the color looks splendid on you, as I knew it would."

"I agree," Sarah chimes in. "I think if I wore a color like that it would make me look washed out."

"Oh, nonsense," Rachael cried. "With your gorgeous blond hair and beautiful skin, you would make any color shine, whereas look at these confounded freckles!" she says, pointing to her own face. "There is nothing to be done about them."

"What do you mean? I love your freckles and gorgeous red hair. When you wear green you put the beauty of the fairest Irish maiden to shame."

"Ye thin' so, do ye?" she demurred, in her best Irish accent.

"Definitely. No one can pull off wearing green tones as well as you can."

"Well, I'll have to admit you're right about that."

When the two women flutter their eyelashes at one another and clink their tea cups, an unlady-like snort escapes me and the three of us are quickly shaking with laughter.

"I don't know what I would do without you two," I say, wiping eyes.

"You will never have to find out," Sarah says, squeezing my hand.

"Yes," Rachael agrees. "Until you can wander freely once more, just consider us your cheer-up squad. Call anytime you need us and we will be here."

"Thank you. That means more to me than you could ever know." I look at them both. "I have been without a mother for years and I've never really had a best friend. Now I have both." The women become teary and my own eyes well up. "Oh, now look what I've done." I smile and we all reach for a tissue. "Sebastian is going to come down and wonder what's wrong with us."

"And we will just tell him it is a woman's prerogative to be emotional," Sarah says. "Tell him it's in the handbook. He can borrow his father's copy."

"And if Devon can't find his, he can borrow my brother's copy. His wife even added notes in the margins."

At that, another fit of giggles takes over.

"And speaking of my brother Jude, I had best be on my way. I promised him I would teach his wife how to cook my specialty, plum pudding."

"Sounds yummy," I tell her.

"Oh, it is," Sarah assures me. "It was a blue ribbon winner at last year's annual Folk Festival."

"How about I bring a dish of it for our next visit?"

"That sounds great." I stand to walk her to the door.

"I'll talk to you later, Rachael," Sarah calls.

"You betcha!"

"Thanks so much for coming, and for the beautiful dress. Did I tell you how much I love it?"

Rachael chuckles merrily. "You did indeed, my dear, and you are very welcome."

Opening the door, I hug her.

"You take care," she calls, waving on the way to her car. I smile, waving back.

"She is a firecracker," I say, joining Sarah again at the table.

"Rachael is an amazing woman, and one of the best people I have ever known."

Thinking about Rachael's sacrifice–the loss of her mate on my behalf, I am again filled with gratitude and grateful to call her friend.

"How has she been able to survive so long without her mate? I thought one mate could not survive without the other."

"Well, normally that is true, and other than the loss of one's mate, nothing but a mortally-fatal wound can kill us.

However, she is still here because of two reasons. First, though James was her true mate, he was killed before they could complete their bonding through ceremony. Though they were in love before he left for the surface, neither of their *Ki Talimai* appeared until he had gone, and while many couples who are already in love are true-mated, most do not fall in love until their marks appear and draw them to one another. They were fortunate that way. However, even though the bond wasn't sealed, Rachael will forever think of James as her husband and true mate. And because the bond wasn't completed–well, because of that and sheer will, Rachael has been able to go on."

"Wow," I whisper, in awe and guilt. Awe because she is so strong and guilt because I am the reason she will probably always be alone. "So there is no chance of her ever falling in love and marrying?"

"She could still fall in love, but fear stands in her way. Say she does marry, and the man she marries is one day led to his true mate through his *Ki Talimai*. Though he would belong to Rachael legally, his heart would never be hers and their lives would be miserable." Sarah pauses, becoming thoughtful for a moment. "Personally I think that if she would allow her heart to open again, *The One* would make a way for her to be happy. You see, since we are immortal, when we die, we rest for a time with *The One* until the appointed day of our return. We don't know when that day will be, nevertheless we know it will happen. Instead of marrying another, Rachael chooses to guard her heart and wait for her mate's return. If she would only leave herself open, since the bonding ceremony never took place, *The One* could erase her mark and remake it for another. Then when James does return, the same can be done for him."

I silently digest what she has told me, feeling sorrow for Rachael being alone, yet grateful the chance for happiness with someone really is hers for the taking.

"And don't worry," Sarah added. "Rachael is not completely alone. She has her brother and his family, as well as her parents now. She spends so much time with them and stays so busy with her shop, she has no time to be down."

"I'm glad." I feel a little better. Not much, but some.

* * *

Before getting out of the car to go into her brother's house, Rachael quickly dries her tears. She really hates these times of weakness. For the most part, she does very well at smiling and exuding happiness and cheer when around others, and most of the time the emotions are genuine, but there are still times when the loneliness and pain touch her all over again.

She especially loathes having these moments around her brother, Jude, because it saddens him, sometimes even angers him. They've had many arguments about James and what could have been. Jude does a good amount of placing blame, and though Rachael tries to help him understand that her mate felt he had no choice, her words do nothing to change his thinking, so she stops talking about it all together and changes the subject.

Truthfully, she has moments of anger, herself. She wishes James had never gone to the surface, that he had stayed with her. But being a guardian was his calling and he would never have turned his back on his duty. He couldn't.

Closing her eyes, she hugs herself, longing for comfort, but the comfort she longs for is unobtainable for now and she again reminds herself that their separation is not permanent.

Come on, get a grip and get over this, she chastises herself. *This has to stop.*

But it is easier said than done.

Twenty-one

As I open the door to see Sarah out, one of the guards turns and hands me a small white envelope.

"This was delivered a few minutes ago. I opened it to make sure it was safe, my lady," he tells me. "But I did not read it."

"Thank you." I wave to Sarah as she reaches her car and smile at the guard before going back in.

"Did you have a good visit?" Sebastian asks, popping one of the small cakes into his mouth and taking a sip of tea from one of the china cups. Watching him, I smile.

"What?"

"Your pinkie finger isn't sticking up properly."

"My what?"

"Your pinkie finger. Didn't you watched any period piece movies on the surface?"

"No," he answers, plucking another cake from the plate.

"Well, if you had, you would know that the proper way to hold a tea cup is by the handle with the pinkie extended."

"Like this?" He maneuvers his long fingers to hold the handle, deftly extending his little finger as he takes a sip.

"Umm, sure," I say, covering my mouth to muffle a giggle, but it's useless.

He scowls a little and puts the cup down, wrapping his hand around it before raising it to his lips. "I'll stick with this way, if that's all right with you."

"It's okay with me, but you get an A for effort."

"Thank you," he says, a sexy grin splitting his face and I laugh. "What is that?" He nods to the envelope in my hand.

"I don't know. One of the guards handed it to me."

"Did he say who delivered it?"

"No. He said he opened it to make sure there was no danger, but he didn't read it."

Sebastian moves to stand next to me while I open it. It is a foil embossed card with the phrase, "Think of You" written in beautiful gold script. I read the card, smiling at the words of encouragement. When I reach the last line, the blood drains from my face. In a flash I feel the breeze of

Sebastian's departure as he zips to the door, returning a second later.

"The guard is gone. I must inform Father and the council."

The guards never leave without waiting for their replacement, and even then they inform us of the change before leaving, which leaves us with one conclusion: this particular guard is now a fugitive and can no longer be trusted. My eyes move to the open note on the table where I dropped it, a cold shudder ripping through my body as I silently reread the final line.

This isn't over, Woman of Prophecy. It will only be over with your death.

* * *

A search for the rogue guard is in progress and a replacement guard is sent. I wait in the now-shaded garden room while Sebastian speaks with all the guards and does a final sweep of the grounds.

I am tired. Not tired physically but emotionally. I'm not afraid, at least not for myself but I worry for our son, for our people, our home, and the completely oblivious world on the surface.

Feeling the baby shift, I softly rub my stomach. "You feel it, too, don't you?" He nudges me as if in answer. "Don't worry, little one. Your daddy and I love you very much. We won't let anything happen to you." Heaving a deep sigh, I close my eyes and imagine myself running across the vast green countryside. As the image plays before me, I briefly recall the feeling of freedom that always comes when I run. I miss that freedom, more so at this moment. I take a deep breath, releasing my cabin fever emotions, and instead, turn my thoughts to the future, determined that it will be one of great joy and peace.

* * *

A band of fifty peace keepers track the traitorous guard deep into the forest. He feels them near but will not allow himself to be caught. He can't betray the sender of the note, so he continues to run. It is pointless, he knows, nevertheless, he keeps going because it gives him time to ponder his choices. Truthfully, he knows he really has no choice save one.

Finally surrounded and seeing no opening for escape, the traitor stops and slowly turns, his eyes scanning the circle of men. Having been trained in the use of the inner power residing in all Challissians, he smiles and closes his eyes, calling upon that power. The surrounding warriors move back, readying their shields to defend his attack. The traitor's hands begin to glow as energy surges through him. He takes a deep breath, pulling the surrounding air into his lungs, and with a mighty grunt, slams his hands against his own chest, the force of the blow knocking him to the ground, killing him instantly.

* * *

Venice, Italy

In a cold, dank room under St. Mark's Basilica, Father Bruno Battiano stands with his head bent low, his arms and legs chained to a stone wall. His face is unrecognizable, his eyes swollen shut, his bloodied nose broken, his cheeks black and blue. For hours, the Urchin has beaten and tortured the priest, but he still won't break.

He knows the cost he will inevitably pay for his silence, but it is a sacrifice he is willing to make. He fulfilled his purpose when he bound the Woman of Prophecy to her true mate, helping to bring about the fulfillment of the prophecy. He'd known after performing the ceremony that his life would be forfeit, that sooner or later the enemy would find him and try to force him to reveal the secret he will take to his grave. He had known all of this, and was all right with it. He still is. Dying is only the beginning of an even greater journey. He is ready for that journey.

In between the beatings, the priest had taken the time to examine his life. Thinking on his mortal existence, his only regret is that he has no family to carry on his name–no wife and child to mourn him after he is gone. He should have converted to another religion where he could have had it all, a congregation to lead and a family. Other than the lack of posterity, he has no other regrets. He has lived a good life.

The priest watches his tormentor approach and squares his shoulders as much as possible.

"I will ask one last time. Where is the home of the ancients?"

Pressing his lips together tightly, he shakes his head, closes his eyes, and awaits his death.

He doesn't wait long.

Twenty-two

The number of guards around our home has doubled, and the closer I get to my delivery date, the more anxious the inhabitants of Challis become. Though I feel the love and concern of all, there is also a tension I don't think ever existed here before. Never before has there been mistrust here, only peace and a feeling of security. I feel like it is all my fault, and though Sebastian, his parents, and the council assure me otherwise, the guilt is still there.

Only two weeks away from delivery, my stomach is huge, but I don't mind. Sebastian continues to tell me I'm beautiful, showering me with gifts for myself and the baby. He is patient and loving, making sure I have everything I need and doing what he can to keep my boredom at bay. We finished decorating the nursery last week, and many times he finds me there, sitting in the rocker, gazing around the room and contemplating our son's future.

The nursery is done in blue, white and gold. The drawers of the light maple chest are filled with clothes and blankets, and afghans fill every shelf in the tall corner cabinet. I crocheted over one hundred of them. I know many will not be used for some time, but it did help to stay busy. Who knows, maybe I will save a few to give as gifts to other expectant mothers in the city. My work will not go to waste.

Holding one of the afghans and examining my handiwork, I look up when Sebastian enters. His expression is grave as he approaches me.

"There is news from the surface."

"What is it?" I don't like the look on his face at all. It can only mean something bad has happened.

He gently takes my arms in his hands, caressing them softly. "It is Father Battiano. Beloved, he has been murdered."

"No," I whisper, not able to believe it, not wanting to hear it. "Was it the Urchin?" I ask tearfully, knowing the answer already.

He nods. "He was tortured, most likely to get the location of our home. But he didn't break. He sacrificed himself for us."

I am too emotional to say anything more. The tears come and he quickly pulls me into his arms, his chest muffling my sobs. That dear sweet man is dead, and I can't stop the guilt tearing through me. People have died, and will die because of me.

No, Celine. It is not your fault. Do not blame yourself. I won't let you.

As I continue to cry, he picks me up and carries me to our room. Soon I am lying on the bed, wrapped in the cradle of his arms.

I'm so tired, Sebastian. I'm so tired of others dying because of me. I cling to him and he holds me tighter.

Listen to me, beloved. Those who die in your service are proud to do so because of the cause for which they fight. They know what is at stake and they do so willingly. We mourn for them and will remember them always because they served selflessly and died with honor. We can't take that away from them.

The tears continue to flow and he pulls me further into himself, the touch of his hands and the warmth of his body slowly soothing my emotions, and I silently accept the comfort he gives. He is right, I know, but it still doesn't make this any easier.

"Did he have family at all?" My voice is strained.

"Sadly, no."

I take a calming breath, getting my emotions under control. "We must tell the people about him. His sacrifice should not be forgotten. *He* must not be forgotten."

"He won't, angel. I promise you he won't."

* * *

Mount St. Helens

The Urchin leader stands before Lord Derth.

"My lord, the priest is dead."

"Of course he is," he replies, with heavy sarcasm. "But the question is, were you able to extract information from him before his life expired?"

"No, my lord."

"So you are telling me you still have nothing?" The tone of the dark lord's voice is both cold and impatient. He has grown tired of excuses. He should have let the Urchin kill her that night in Italy instead of ordering that she be brought back to him.

The longer it takes to locate the woman who carries the means to his death in her womb, the less time he has left before her spawn is born. He cannot tolerate failure, for to do so will surely be his demise. The Urchins–the so-called threat to the human race, grow more useless by the day, and he is ready to do away with the leader and replace him with another more suited for the job. But the Urchin's next words change the path of his thoughts and bring a smile to his face.

"We've had a breakthrough, my lord. The team in the north made an exchange and have collected the traded information. We know where the ancient ones reside."

Twenty-three

Two miles east in a secluded grove of olive trees sits a missile containing just enough C-4 to demolish the small mansion with no problem. The bomb is constructed with the best materials, the ingredients super-strength for efficiency. It is aimed at its target with total accuracy. In another thirty seconds there will be a large gaping crater where the house now stands, making this officially the second violent act to be perpetrated in the so-called peaceful world of Challis.

It hadn't been hard to acquire the ingredients for the bomb. The asking price had been steep but easily met, and the mode in which the transaction between the inner and outer earth was made had indeed been clever. Eagles are not known for being docile creatures, but training the massive bird had been easy.

The Challissian people aren't as thorough as they assume they are. In less than a minute they will regret that fact.

* * *

"You know, we still need to decide on a name."

Turning from the nursery window where I have been standing for a while now, I manage to smile. I am still saddened over Father Battiano's death, and this is Sebastian's way of steering my thoughts toward happier things. I love him so much for that.

"There is a name I have been considering for a while now, but so much has been going on, I keep forgetting to run it by you. Of course, you probably already know, having twenty-four-hour access to my thoughts and all."

He smiles slyly. "True, but why don't you tell me anyway, just to make sure I know."

"Well, since naming him Sebastian will be kind of confusing, I thought we could use your middle name and your father's name. What do you think of Antonio Devon?"

"I think it is perfect," he says, taking my hands in his, raising them to his lips. "Father will be surprised and deeply honored."

"Okay, Antonio Devon it is. It's only fitting that I name him after the two men I love most in the world."

"Thank you, *cara*."

I smile and run a hand over my stomach. "Did you hear that, baby? How do you like your name, Antonio?" In answer, my stomach rolls and I receive a strong kick in the ribs. I laugh at our son's response. "I guess you like it, huh?"

Antonio continues to kick, each one growing stronger until they border on pain, which has never happened before.

Leave.

The soft voice in my mind startles me.

"Did you say something?"

"No," Sebastian answers, puzzled.

No, of course it wasn't him, I muse. *I know his voice as well as my own. Still, if it wasn't Sebastian, then who . . .*

As the voice comes again, my eyes meet his and we both gasp.

Leave, Mama! Leave now!

The explosion is instant and rocks the entire city.

* * *

"What in the blazes was that?"

Aaron looks at the guard, his face grave. "I don't know, but we cannot leave our post." His bushy brow furrows. "I am sure someone will bring us word soon." He braces himself against a tree as an onslaught of questions from guards all around the north opening enters his mind with force.

Men, until we have a report, remain at your posts. I have a feeling the enemy will be upon us soon, possibly in the next day or two. We must stand alert and ready.

Yes, sir! a chorus of voices reply.

The time for preparation is drawing to an end. Their people have looked forward to the coming event for centuries, have anticipated the birth of the child who will banish Lord Derth with the intake of his very first breath.

Aaron completely severs his mind from the others. Leaning against the tree, he closes his eyes to commune with the being who is the beginning and end of all things.

Oh, Great One *who knows all, we your people, both in the world and on it, need your help, your guidance and protection. The time of war and wonder is upon us. Our lives are in your hands. I give mine freely, for it was you who gave me life. My sword and my soul are yours.*

He opens his eyes as a warm burst of air flows around and through him, and in this brief moment he knows all will be set right.

* * *

The assassin watches from the grove as the granite and crystal building explodes, shattering into a million pieces, forcing a great cloud of smoke to ascend high above the city. There is no question that the inhabitants of the home are no more. Success is in the air, so tangible one can taste it, touch it. The assassin watches people run to the scene of death and carnage. Satisfaction is present in abundance and partaken in gluttonous abandon. Restitution has been made–a life for a life. A long-awaited goal has at last been met.

Now to prepare my family for evacuation, for death is at the door.

* * *

With tears running down his face, Devon holds his wife close, her wet face pressed against his shoulder as he watches the investigative disaster team search through the wreckage for signs of life. All twelve guards have been found, five of them having died instantly from the blast. The rest are seriously injured, but are already beginning to recover from their wounds.

The disaster team finishes quickly, and under President Simon's orders, tells no one of their findings.

Tears are shed by the entire city and thick despair settles over the land. In the history of Challis, nothing like this has ever happened, and the people don't know how to handle it. What will they do now? If the prophecy is not fulfilled, if the golden child is not born, what will become of them? Nothing can stop the enemy from destroying them now.

Peace keepers have been dispatched all over the city to find the person or persons responsible.

The citizens are instructed to return to their homes. They do so with heads hanging low and hearts devoid of hope.

Twenty-four

The cave we inhabit is guarded by two mammoths, a group of five enormous black panthers and five Bengal tigers. The animals are just as protective of me as Sebastian. We've often communed with them whenever we've come out to the countryside and they understand the importance of the child I carry. The bear in whose home we are staying willingly gave up his living space and sought shelter elsewhere.

Between the two of us, we've turned the once dark cavern into a cozy hideaway. A large, down comforter-covered bed sits against the far wall. A rustic, brown leather sofa is situated across from the bed and a large braided rug stretches out between them. I still find it unreal at times that I can simply will things into existence.

We have food, water, light, and even a few of my favorite books. Anything else can be created as we need it.

I lay on the bed with my head on Sebastian's shoulder, his arms curled around me, and lightly rub my stomach as we silently marvel at what has just taken place.

Our unborn child spoke to us! He literally warned us to flee and we barely escaped. The explosion had come fast and we felt its impact a mile away from the house. Someone still wanted me dead, enough to blow up our home along with anyone in or near it. It couldn't have been anyone from the surface, because both entrances are being monitored and guarded around the clock. My senses are fine-tuned enough now to sense danger, but this was done at a distance. It had to be.

Now our beautiful home is gone and our people most likely believe we are dead, which according to Sebastian is good and bad–good because the assassin will believe he or she has been successful, and bad because the people will lose hope. However, Sebastian has telepathically contacted President Simon to let him know we are alive. The president agreed that our escape should be kept silent for now. He didn't want to know our location, only that we were safe.

Little Antonio has been extremely active but is now calm and still, except for a hand or foot prodding every now and then. He is also settled lower in my stomach now, readying himself for birth, which means labor could start at any time. I am both excited and afraid. I had thought our son's birth would happen in the comfort of our home where everything is light, airy and peaceful. I also hoped Sarah would be present. Taking in our surroundings I decide that two out of three isn't bad. At least it is airy and peaceful.

My eyes fall on a small shelf that sits a little ways from the bed, filled with towels, cloths, oils, herbs, extra gowns, baby blankets and clothes, and other things I will need for the birth. A large vase of water sits next to it. Sebastian will deliver the baby and has made sure we have everything we will need. Though neither of us have ever had any experience in this area, Sebastian is confident he can do what needs to be done, and though delivery will not be painful like it is for women on the surface, it will still be exhausting work. I'll take exhaustion over pain any day.

Are you well, beloved?

Adjusting my head, I look into his eyes. *I'm all right. But I don't think it will be long. I can feel the change in my body, like it's readying itself. Your mother told me it would be like that, that I would know.*

I feel the change as well. I feel a new strength in you. He smiles. *The healer said our women are at their most vulnerable when carrying a child, but you are not like the rest. You are far more gifted.*

I smile back. *Do you think?*

I do.

Sighing, I place a hand on his solid chest over his heart. He lays his hand over mine, holding it there, and feeling the calm rhythm beating against my palm, I snuggle closer.

Tell me more about when you were a boy.

* * *

Sebastian shifts a little, placing his free hand behind his head, and stares up at the jagged ceiling as a number of memories flow through his mind at once. His childhood had been a happy one, filled with love, laughter and some hard-learned lessons that he wouldn't trade for anything.

"When I was ten, there were a couple of boys at my school who were constantly trying to provoke a fight with me. I was about five-foot-eleven and towered over all the other children at school, which made me an easy target for the two bully boys."

Celine whistles and he can see her visualizing his height back then. "I assume they wanted to prove their manhood and toughness by beating up the biggest kid at school?" she muses.

"You assume correctly. It was very hard for me, not because I was afraid, but because I knew I could beat them, even hurt them permanently. My powers began to emerge at nine years old. My father tried to train me as much as he could, but I think he and Mother knew even then, that they would eventually have to bring me to Challis, not only because they would come to miss their home, but because they recognized that my powers were manifesting faster than any other child they'd seen of our people. I would need more training than Father could give me."

"I'm guessing *The One* gave you more power and strength because he knew you would be chosen to guard the Woman of Prophecy."

"A fact I came to know over ten years later." He pauses and turns to her, caressing her cheek. "If I had only known then how much I would be blessed now . . ." His words are silenced as her warm mouth raises to meets his.

Celine clears her throat loudly. "Back to the story."

He laughs. "All right, back to the story. One day both boys jumped me in an alley on my way home from school. They pounded away at me and it didn't hurt at all. Their punches had absolutely no affect on me."

"Really?"

"Really, but this made them even madder, so they kept going with no intention of stopping until they caused me at least some pain. Finally, I decided that I'd had it. So, clearing all anger from my mind, I grabbed them both, holding the collar of each boy in separate hands and lifted them off the ground. I told them to never try that again or they would be sorry. Then I knocked their heads together and dropped them on the ground. They were dazed and holding there heads. Seeing that they were okay, I walked away. On the way home I began to feel guilty, and by the time I reached my front door, I was sad and afraid–sad because I allowed myself to be provoked into fighting, and afraid because I knew how disappointed my parents would be in me."

She softly caresses the muscles of his arm. "And were they?"

He chuckles, a look of melancholy filling his eyes and touching his smile. "I was sure they would be, but they weren't. After I explained what happened and how sorry I was for giving in to violence, my mother simply kissed my cheek and went to the kitchen. My father sat down beside me, put his arm around me and said he was proud of me. I couldn't believe it and I asked him why. He told me that after going through half the school year being taunted and provoked, any other kid my size with even a small portion of my abilities would have squashed them both like little cockroaches. I had done my best to avoid confrontation, but a fight was inevitable, and because it was done in self defense with no anger and I truly felt sorrow afterward, I did nothing wrong. He said I was, at only ten years old, more of a man than the boys could ever hope to be."

"Wow," she whispers. He sends her flashes of the special memory residing in his heart and feels her awe.

"Even if you hadn't sent me the visual, I could still see and hear your father speaking those words to you. He's an amazing man. And you are just like him."

"I try to be," he says humbly.

She moves to kiss him again and he meets her half way. "Believe me, you are," she whispers against his lips.

Moaning softly, he holds her close. How he loves this woman! She is the very air he breathes, the literal life force that flows through his veins. He can literally feel her moving inside his soul, and as he takes her hand in his, weaving his fingers through hers, their *Ki Talimai* burn, sending heat racing through his entire body. He finally draws back and presses his forehead to hers, slowing his breathing. He can't mate with her now, not with the birth so close, but oh, how he wants her! And drawing back a little more, he sees the same need burning in her clear hazel eyes. He kisses her again and her thoughts flow to him, bringing him comfort.

I love you, Sebastian. We will again share our love in the merging of bodies soon.

Twenty-five

The young man is nervous and a little frightened as he stands before President Simon and his counselors. At only fourteen, he never dreamed anything like this would happen to him, that he would be needed to assist in an investigation into the murder of the Woman of Prophecy. He had been both saddened and shocked when his mother told him about the bomb that demolished the home of Lady Celine and her brave true mate. Sebastian Giovanni had become a legend to the people of Challis, both young and old, and every young man wanted to *be* him.

Now that the prophecy is no longer able to be fulfilled, what will become of his people, his world? This question has rolled through his mind over and over. And the fact that he might have helped to prevent their loss tears him up inside. After all, he has seen and heard many things.

And he knows about the fruit basket.

"John," Devon says, startling him, "it's all right." He gives the boy's shoulder a gentle squeeze. "Just tell the president what you told me. You will not be blamed for anything because none of this is your fault." Devon's voice is soft and full of understanding, devoid of any of the turmoil he'd felt earlier, because of his new-found knowledge that Celine and Sebastian are safe. "Just tell the truth."

John straightens his shoulders, raising to his full height of six-feet-eight inches, then takes a deep breath and begins.

"Trevor Walton is my best friend. If we are not at my house we are usually at his. His family is really nice, especially his Aunt Rachael. She's pretty and I like being there when she's visiting." He pauses, realizing what he'd said and a deep blush flushes his face when a few chuckles come from the council. He cuts his eyes to Devon who is trying to conceal the grin spreading across his face. The boy clears his throat and faces the council again.

"Anyway, the past few times she was there, I saw her crying on her brother's shoulder. She told him how much she still missed her mate and how lonely she feels sometimes. He told her that one day everything would be okay. The last time I went over and she was there, she was happy and talked to Mr. and Mrs. Walton about Lady Celine. She told them what a lovely and kind lady she was. She said she wanted to do something nice for her and mentioned sending her a fruit basket." He hesitates, looking at Devon who urges him to continue.

"She was going to pick out some fruit, put it in a basket, and take it to Lady Celine, but her brother . . . I mean Mr. Walton, said she should just have it delivered. Mrs. Walton asked why and Mr. Walton said Miss Rachael shouldn't go over unannounced, that it might not sit well with Lady Celine. Both ladies agreed and Miss Rachael went to buy the fruit. Mr. Walton said to bring it back there, that way they could add some fresh pears from their orchard to the basket and he would have someone else deliver it, maybe even himself. I was still there when Miss Rachael returned. John and I went up to his room to play a game of chess. A few minutes later I heard my name being called. When I went back downstairs, the basket was sitting on the kitchen table filled to the brim with fruit, and the Walton's pears were mixed in.

"Mr. Walton suggested that I deliver it. That way, it would be a surprise." John smiles. "I was excited to get to see Lady Celine up close, so I said I would take it. Because my shirt was a little dirty, Trevor let me borrow one of his good ones. Mr. Walton even let me take his car. He told me

Miss Rachael wanted it to be anonymous and not to say who it was from. She agreed and I left. I delivered the basket and went back to the Walton's. A little while later we heard from a neighbor that Lady Celine had been poisoned."

Bead's of sweat appear on John's forehead as he remembers that day, as well as the thought that ran through his head the very moment he heard the news. He swipes an arm across his forehead.

"Why did you not tell someone?" President Simon asks, apparently reading the boy's thoughts.

"Because I just couldn't believe the Waltons would do anything to hurt Lady Celine, especially Miss Rachael. She was very fond of her and had even wanted to take the basket herself. She was in tears when we heard. I wondered about Mr. Walton, but I put the thought out of my mind."

The president nods, accepting his earnest reply. "Go on," he says softly.

"Well, after that, Miss Rachael and Lady Celine became friends, and Miss Rachael always check on her through her friend, who is Lady Celine's mother-in-law. But I guess you already knew the last part." Devon smiles, patting his shoulder for him to continue. "Well, one day when I was at the Walton's, I heard Miss Rachael and Mr. Walton arguing. She was telling him how grateful she was for Lady Celine and how happy she was that the lives of her ancestors had been spared so Lady Celine could be here to fulfill the prophecy. He asked her how she could be grateful that her mate is dead. Mrs. Walton told him that wasn't what Miss Rachael meant at all. Then Miss Rachael left the house crying. Mrs. Walton shook her head and left the room. Mr. Walton stood there for a minute, then left, saying he had some things to take care of. Trevor and I kind of shrugged our shoulders at each other and went to my house."

John is quiet for a moment and watches the counselors scribble down a few notes.

Devon squeezes John's shoulder. "Go on."

John nervously wipes his hands against his leggings. He doesn't want to tell them the next part, but he has no choice.

"Well, sir . . . this morning when I went to get Trevor for classes, I heard his parents arguing. Mr. Trevor said he was tired of his sister being alone and if her mate had not been assigned to protect Lady Celine's family, he and Miss Rachael could have been bound, and she would have a family of her own. Then he said one day things will be made right. We left for class after that, but I saw the look on Mr. Walton's face before we left. He looked mad, real mad." John takes a deep breath. "And that's it. I haven't seen Trevor or his family since."

President Simon approaches John and clasps his hand. "Thank you for coming forward, John. You have helped us more than you know."

"Yes, sir." He lowers his eyes. "I just wish I had come forward sooner."

"You weren't convinced anything was wrong. You did not want to accuse an innocent man of murder, which is completely understandable." The president turns to confer with his counselors.

"You did well," Devon whispers to John.

"What will they do?" John asks.

"I imagine they will have him brought in for questioning." He sees the distressed look on John's face. "Don't worry," he says, squeezing his shoulder again. "Your name will never be mentioned, and if he is innocent they will know."

Twenty-six

Two peace keepers knock on the Walton's door while an additional eight spread out around the grounds. When the door opens, the men come face to face with Jude Walton.

"Mr. Walton, we need you to come with us to the town hall for questioning."

Jude's brow furrows. "What is this about?" His voice is calm.

"The council has strong reason to believe you were involved in the murders of Sebastian and Celine Giovanni."

"You cannot be serious!" Gwenyth Walton cries from behind him. "Who would make such an accusation?"

"We are not at liberty to answer that."

Gwenyth's mouth begins to move, but nothing comes out.

"Come with us, Mr. Walton."

"No!" Gwenyth cries. "He doesn't have to go anywhere with you!" She grabs her husband's sleeve. "Tell them you won't go!"

Jude places a calming hand over hers. "It's all right. I will go and be back before you know it." Saying nothing else, he goes with the men, leaving his wife tearfully staring after him.

* * *

Jude is calm as he sits before the president and his counselors. He notices Devon Giovanni has joined them. If the council thinks the man'a presence will intimidate him, they are wrong.

Before the questioning begins, Jude closes his mind completely, preventing his thoughts from being read in any way. He stares at the men sitting around the table, forming an arch, and steels himself against the coming onslaught of questions, determined not to be intimidated at all. He will show no weakness. Let them do what they may with him, it really doesn't matter anymore.

President Simon leans forward. "Mr. Walton, let me start with a blunt question. Do you or have you ever blamed Lady Celine for the death of your sister's true mate?"

Saying nothing, Jude focuses on a painting high on the wall behind the council, keeping his eyes there.

"Have you had any contact at all with anyone on the surface?"

Again, he says nothing.

"Did you have anything to do with the death of the Woman of Prophecy and her mate?"

Nothing.

"Do you know anything about the poisoned fruit delivered to Lady Celine's home?"

Nothing.

"Have you nothing to say?"

Nothing.

"Will you not cooperate at all?"

Nothing.

Jude finally drops his eyes to the counselors as they speak softly to one another. They have no proof, no evidence, so he will continue to say nothing. He knows they will most likely hold him for a day or two, then have no choice but to let him go. He will just bide his time.

Feeling a set of eyes on him, he turns, meeting the piercing gaze of Devon Giovanni. The man isn't participating in the conversation with the council, or even paying attention to them for that matter. Jude tries to look away but is unable to for a moment. It is finally Devon who looks away, but there is something different in his expression, something that puts Jude on edge, though he masks it well.

"President, may I have a private word with you, please?" Devon asks, standing.

"Certainly." The two men exit the room.

Jude remains expressionless as he watches them leave. His face is still a mask of calm, belying what he feels inside, but he continues to shield his thoughts.

There is nothing to worry about, he affirms. *They know nothing, and they will get nothing from me.*

Both men are expressionless when they return. They quietly take their seats at the table and President Simon begins questioning again.

"Mr. Walton, do you know of anyone else who has ill feelings toward Lady Celine?"

Jude says nothing. His eyes have returned to the painting, though there is a slight twitch in his brow as he does so. The reaction does not go unnoticed.

The president sighs. "You are protecting someone, aren't you? Someone close."

Still nothing, but there is another twitch.

"Who are you protecting, Mr. Walton?"

Still nothing, but there is a quick clinch of the jaw.

The president leans back in his chair and stares at him quietly for one, two, three, four, five minutes. During this time the only sound in the room is the ticking of the clock on the wall behind Jude.

Jude continues to stare at the painting, but he can feel himself wavering a bit. The longer the president stares at him, the more unsettled he becomes. He feels his shield beginning to slip but promptly locks it in place again.

The brief slip is all the president needed. He finally sits forward again, resting his clasped hands on the table.

"I apologize for the strained silence," he begins. "A period of silence is good for the soul, you see. It helps a person think better, and I have come to some conclusions of my own. Shall I share them with you?" Not waiting for, nor expecting a reply, he forges ahead. "You are indeed protecting someone, Mr. Walton, but the question is *who* are you protecting? Now, one guess is completely obvious."

Jude still says nothing.

"It is no secret that your sister Rachael was deeply hurt when her true mate, James, was killed while protecting Lady Celine's ancestors. They hadn't been able to complete their bonding and your sister has been alone ever since. She still struggles sometimes, does she not?"

Unconsciously balling his hands into fists, Jude continues to stare at the painting.

"It would be hard not to blame Lady Celine. If James hadn't been assigned to protect her ancestors, he would still be alive, and he and Rachael would have completed their bonding. It would be difficult not to be bitter, wouldn't it? She could have easily taking her revenge out on Lady Celine, poisoned her and somehow acquired the parts and ingredients to make a bomb, or even employed someone else to do it. All her cheeriness and friendliness could have been an act. She would be the obvious culprit . . . but she isn't."

Jude's eyes move to the president's as he continues.

"Rachael Walton was hurt, yes, and I'm sure she still hurts from time to time, but Rachael doesn't have a malicious bone in her body. She is a good person, completely without guile, and she truly cares about Lady Celine, a fact that does not make you happy. You two have had arguments over her kind feelings toward Lady Celine, so the murderer isn't your sister." He pauses, staring at him intently. "It isn't you, either. So if it isn't you or your sister, and you are not protecting her, then who *are* you protecting?"

Jude runs a nervous hand through his hair, suddenly finding it hard to keep his thoughts shielded.

"Your wife hasn't been too happy with the discontent between you and your sister, has she? Every time you and Rachael argue, every time she witnesses Rachael's pain and sees her tears, it upsets her, doesn't it?"

"My wife has nothing to do with this!" Jude explodes before he can stop himself.

The president's eyes are sad. "She has everything to do with it, Mr. Walton. And the fact that this is the first question you've responded to during the entire time you have been here tells me with absolute certainty she has everything to do with it."

Jude closes his eyes and lowers his head, the pain of his wife's betrayal piercing his heart all over again. He is unable to stop the tears from filling his eyes and falling down his face. If he had only known . . . Feeling a gentle hand on his shoulder, he looks up to find the president kneeling beside him, his own eyes wet.

"When did you find out it was your wife, Jude?"

Prompted by the gentleness of the president's voice and the love emanating from the man, Jude answers. Feeling Devon's gaze burning into him, he keeps his eyes averted from the his face, concentrating on the president's.

"This morning, we quarreled. I went up to my study to cool down. I took a few moments to meditate and ponder the things I'd said. Feeling better, I went back down to apologize to her only to find that she'd left without a word to anyone. I decided to sit in the living room and wait for her, hoping she would be back soon. Half an hour later, I heard this loud explosion. A huge cloud of black smoke rose in the air. The streets were instantly crawling with people running toward the smoke. But I stayed home, wanting to be there when Gwenyth came back." His voice breaks. "Soon people were walking back, most of them in tears, with the news of Lady Celine's murder, as well as her true mate. Someone had blown up their home, killing them and some of their guards. I was in shock, couldn't believe it. I mean, I had been angry about the loss of Rachael's mate on Lady Celine's behalf, but I never wanted her hurt. I never wanted her killed.

"A while later, I went back into the house. Gwenyth was standing at the kitchen sink, scrubbing her hands. Even as I approached her, she hadn't noticed me there, she just continued to scrub with this slight smile on her face . . . and in that moment, I knew. I said, "Woman, what have you done?" She just continued to smile and said, "I've made things right–a life for a life.""

Jude shakes his head sadly. "She finally turned to me, saw my expression, and began to cry. I led her to the living room sofa, where she told me everything–about poisoning the fruit, constructing the bomb, and how she'd accomplished all of this by using an eagle to ferry both messages and supplies back and forth from here to the surface. She blamed Lady Celine for everything, for the arguments, the unhappiness, Rachael's loneliness. She said it was only fitting that Lady Celine's life be taken to pay for the loss of James. She had become so bitter, she gave no thought to how many other lives would be destroyed in the process. She begged me to protect her and I said I would. And what a great fool I have been, about everything." He meets the president's eyes. "With Lady Celine no longer living, the prophecy can't be fulfilled, because there will be no golden child to destroy the enemy and bring peace to the world."

"The prophecy will still come to pass," the president say softly.

Jude's eyes widen. "What . . . but how?"

"We felt it was best to keep this information confidential until we discovered the assassin. Lady Celine and her mate escaped. They are safe."

"Safe?" he whispers, unable to believe it.

"They are safe. We can now inform the rest of the city that the Woman of Prophecy and her mate were not in their home when it exploded."

Smiling sadly, Jude said, "But I haven't told you the wost of what Gwenyth has done."

"What else has she done?"

He swallows hard. "She . . . she paid for the supplies with information. She told the enemy about Challis. They know where we are." Seeing the president's eyes widen, he presses his head in his hands and sobs bitterly.

President Simon stands, turning to his counselors, his voice surprisingly calm. "Send a squad of peace keepers to the Walton's home and pick up Gwenyth." One of the counselors immediately complies. "Devon, contact Aaron and tell him to make ready all the squads. Tell him the enemy has the exact coordinates of Challis. They must not get through."

Devon nods, quickly taking his leave.

"I will contact Sebastian and fill him in." With the warrior's connection to the animals, President Simon is sure the powerful guardian will have their help and will protect his mate with everything in him.

"I would like to go with them to pick up my wife," Jude says. "Please."

President Simon nods. "You may go."

* * *

Staring at the portrait she took with her husband and son, Gwenyth swallows her emotion, blinking back the pressing tears. She would lose everything now. She had gambled and lost. She thought their problems would be over with Celine and her mate gone, that Jude and Rachael would finally be able have peace between them again.

She had done it for them.

Nothing is turning out the way she had hoped. She had given her all, but it hadn't been enough.

Hearing a knock at the door, she takes a deep breath.

Gweynth's face is expressionless when she opens the door and comes face to face with her husband and two peace keepers. She had known they would come, and in a way, she is glad they discovered the truth. As much as she wanted to let Jude take the blame, when all was said and done, she had known in the end she couldn't because she loves him too much to offer him up as a sacrifice. If they had not come for her, she had been prepared to go to them and confess. She is not sorry for what she did, only that Jude got caught in the middle.

She finally meets her husband's eyes.

I'm so sorry, he begins. *I tried to . . .*

It is all right, she interrupts, tears now filling her eyes. *I love you, Jude. Take care of our son. He will not understand. Tell him I love him.*

Gwenyth . . .

She shakes her head. There is nothing else to say. Leaning forward, she kisses him, then steps around him and leaves with the peace keepers.

Twenty-seven

Mount St. Helens

Standing in the middle of the dimly-lit medical room, Lord Derth looks up at his latest created Urchin. Part man, part machine, Lord Derth has been harvesting both weak and deathbed humans for years, implanting mechanical parts and inserting deadly toxins the creatures can use to kill their victims. Then newly-created Urchins are trained in the art of warfare, taught to use weapons made especially for them, schooled in the ways to administer their deadly poison, and incapacitate with the acidic mucus they produce. They are pure killing machines, bred for no other purpose than the annihilation of man.

With sadistic pleasure, he gazes upon his final masterpiece. At seven feet tall, the new Urchin towers above the rest. Built from the same blueprint, this Urchin possesses advanced training, able to take on a dozen of its kind at once, incapacitating them all. Lord Derth has had to replace many due to the training of this one, but it has been well worth it, for his new killing machine is unstoppable.

In another five minutes, the Urchin's regeneration will be complete. Then it will join the others and lead the killing army to the north, where, thanks to one of Challis' traitorous citizens (they can't even trust their own people) they will enter the center of the earth and destroy the Woman of Prophecy along with the rest of his enemies. Until recently, he had wanted the pleasure of killing her himself, but that desire is no longer at the forefront. Now he just wants her dead, period. Today it will finally happen.

He smiles, visualizing the victory. It will be sweet.

* * *

North polar opening

After contacting warriors in Russia, Greenland, and Canada, as well as troops guarding the south opening, Aaron shakes his head sadly, wondering how one person could be so blind and stupid, she would put so many lives at risk to satisfy her revenge on one, and the Woman of Prophecy no less! Until now, he would never have believed it of one of his people, that a Challissian would put her own blood lust before the safety of her own people. He can't even fathom such a thing!

Shaking his head once more, he clears the anger from his mind, concentrating on what lies before them. Their orders had been clear. No one must be allowed to enter the opening. New warriors are arriving from Challis this very minute. Hundreds of them. Every inch of the opening must be guarded. The warriors must provide as much coverage as possible. The birth of the golden child is very close, and if they can hold the Urchins off long enough, the birth will bring them instant victory. The prayers of many are centered around this. Surely *The One* hears their heartfelt pleas and will stand with them.

* * *

The assassin is in custody, but it still isn't safe enough to come out of hiding, for war is drawing near as we speak.

I understand, President.

How is Celine?

She is a little tired but doing well.

Do you have everything you need?

Yes, we are prepared and anxiously awaiting our son's arrival.

We are as well. What a joyful moment that will be. Stay safe and may The One *watch over you.*

And you.

Sebastian continues to softly stroke Celine's bare stomach, giving her a sip of water every ten minutes or so. She is tired but feels fine otherwise. Since he'd kept his mind open to hers during his telepathic communication with the president, there is no need to repeat what had been said.

"It will be soon," she says softly. "I can feel it."

"I feel it as well, beloved."

She closes her eyes. "Tell me more about the things you plan to do with our son."

"Well," he begins, thoughtful for a moment. "When he is old enough, I will teach him how to connect with the animals, maybe even take him for a ride on a mammoth." When she laughs, he says, "I'm serious. Mammoth riding is an art form."

"Really? And you've ridden one?"

"Many. I rode them all the time as a child and quite a few times as an adult."

"Okay, this is something I will have to see one day."

"And you shall. I will also teach him how to use his powers properly when they begin to emerge. How to discern between good and evil, right and wrong. How to laugh and enjoy life, and look for the good in everything. How to be fiercely protective of family. How to be strong in love, true to his mate, and love unconditionally." He pauses.

"But I can do none of these things without *The One* guiding me."

"And he will," she says. "Just as he guides you now." She covers her mouth, yawning.

"You are growing more tired, my heart. You should sleep for a while." He pulls the blanket up over her. "I won't leave your side."

"Okay," she softly replies without protest.

Ever alert to his surroundings, he holds her close, wrapping her in his warmth.

* * *

Stand ready, men! Aaron commands. *They are here!*

The attack is fast and brutal, the cries of war echoing in every direction. Thoroughly trained to defend themselves against every Urchin weapon, including shielding against their venom, the Challissian warriors fight with everything they have. Their indestructible swords pierce hearts, decapitate arms, heads and legs. There is much blood, more than any of the men have ever seen at once. Even after losing a body part, some of the Urchins continue to fight until they can no longer stand, in which case the warriors speedily finish them off.

Though the warriors are trained to use many weapons, each man is extra-gifted in the use of a specific weapon. Some are trained to wield a sword well. For some it is the bow and arrow. For some it is knives, throwing stars, blow darts, the ax or spear, or in Sebastian's case, all of them.

But Aaron's weapon of choice is a four-foot-long pick ax. Wielding it up, down, and sideways, each blow lands with accuracy. He bears cuts and bruises on his chest, arms and legs, but he gives as much as he gets and eventually overpowers his foes. All around him Urchins drop like flies.

In the midst of the battle, something fast zips by Aaron at an incredible speed, but there is no time or opportunity to stop it.

Sebastian! he telepathically shouts, *one made it past us! Stand ready! I repeat, stand ready!*

Understood, comes the fervent answer.

After disposing of the first wave of Urchins, a second wave attacks and these creatures are even stronger than the first. The warriors continue to fight with abandon, suffering a fair amount of injuries and losing several men on every side. But even with the blood and lives lost, they continue to overtake the enemy. The battle lasts for the better part of an hour and the Challissians are exhausted, but they keep fighting until the last Urchin is down.

All captains report! Aaron calls.

One by one the men answer, reporting how many of their own are dead. The total comes to forty. Forty out of four hundred. Aaron had expected lives to be lost, but it still saddens him to lose even the forty.

Continue to stand guard, he orders and each captain complies. Everything in him wants to go down to assist Sebastian, but he can't leave his men. There has been no word of the child's birth, and he can only pray that Celine is protected.

"May *The One* be with them."

Twenty-eight

Standing on a large rock, I see nothing but ocean for miles. Massive waves break against the rock, the water turning frothy before receding. I am completely alone, staring out over the deep waters. The wind whips my hair away from my face, pressing my dress back, making it cling to me. Somewhere I hear my name being whispered in the wind and the voice is familiar to me. As it slowly grows in volume, I recognize it–the voice of my true mate calling to me.

Just as I open my mouth to call back, I find myself standing on the edge of a large, gaping hole. Looking down, I see nothing below. I stand silently listening, and after a moment, I hear sounds coming from the dark opening. Animals are calling out, and it's like they are calling to one another. In the midst of it all, I again hear my true mate's voice, only this time he is not calling to me.

This time his voice is filled with the sound of war–war and exhaustion.

Then a light appears, illuminating the hole, and I see him. He is bloody and battered, his shirt practically hanging from his body, exposing long cuts and gashes on his chest and torso. The creature he is fighting is massive, almost as tall as my mate. It looks half human, half machine, and its reflexes are just as fast as my mate's.

It is injured as well, but, like my mate, that doesn't slow it at all. They continue to fight, blocking each others' blows. The creature spews an acidic substance from its mouth. My mate produces a shield, easily blocking it before the poison can touch his skin. Lightening fast, the creature reaches out with one of its long claws. My mate leaps back and quickly produces a bow, releasing an arrow in less than a second. The arrow pierces one of the creature's eyes and it staggers back a bit before pulling the arrow out.

Three enormous leopards suddenly appear and attack the creature, knocking it to the ground. The creature opens its claws and catches one of them around the neck, severing the head from the body. The two remaining leopards bite and scratch the grossly-deformed body. It spews venom on both and they fall to the ground, rolling back and forth as the deadly poison eats through their fur and gradually consumes their bodies.

I cover my mouth and tears roll down my face as I mourn for the brave animals. One of my tears falls down the hole, landing on the creature's bald head.

Pausing for a few seconds, it slowly looks up and sees me, then starts crawling up the side of the hole.

"No!" I hear my mate roar, coming after the creature. He grabs one of the legs and yanks it back down. It turns, ripping his chest with one of its jagged claws and I scream.

I come awake with a gasp.

Finding myself alone, I sit up, my ears instantly picking up loud sounds coming from outside the cave. One of the sounds stands out clearly–that of tearing flesh. It matches the one I just heard in my dream . . . only it wasn't a dream.

Somehow, through my subconscious, I've witnessed the entire fight.

Sebastian! I anxiously call. He does not answer me.

Sebastian!

I am about to stand when a sudden jolt of energy shoots through me, causing my flesh to tingle. The sensation spreads over my limbs. The baby is pressing, but I am unable to ignore the silent call of my mate. I try to fight the urge, knowing he would want me to stay here for the sake of the baby, but the call of his life force to mine is stronger. Energy begins to burn through me and before I know it, I am at the cave entrance.

The sight of my mate, bloody and tired, causes a feeling I have never felt before to enter every nerve of my body. It flows from deep within me, building with each passing second. The power moves down my arms into my hands, and before I can comprehend what is happening, I leap from the cave entrance, vaulting over the animals guarding the opening, springing high in the air. Sebastian's head jerks toward me as I arch toward them. The Urchin turns to defend himself but isn't quick enough. As my closed fist lands hard against its chest, power explodes from my hand, sending the creature reeling backwards in the air. The body lands with a thump over a hundred yards away. But our combined relieved sighs are premature. We turn as the Urchin sits up. Just as it attempts to stand, two Tyrannosaurus Rex release a battle cry behind us. They charge forward, stomping the creature into the ground. Within seconds, it disintegrates. And within those same seconds, all energy leaves me. Sebastian catches me before I hit the ground.

"Celine!" I look at him and smile. There is worry in his eyes and voice, but there is also wonder. Lifting my hand to his chest, I touch his already healing skin. He smiles back. "You've been holding out on me."

"I've been holding out on *me*. I've never felt anything like that before."

"Well, I'm glad your new-found ability decided to manifest itself now. I was in desperate need of a moment to regenerate in order to do that same magic trick. I've never been so depleted of energy before. It looks like Lord Derth saved his best for last."

"It looks that . . ." A sudden hard pressure followed by a gush of wetness cuts off my words.

In a flash, we are in the cave and I am changed into a gown, sitting in a newly-produced birthing chair. Sebastian is kneeling before me with is hands on my knees, looking up at me through shining eyes.

The moment we have anticipated and done our best to prepare for is finally here. There is no danger near, no Urchins to try and stop what is about to happen. No more opposition to fight against, no threats to my life or the life of our child.

"It's really happening, isn't it?"

"Yes, beloved," he answers, looking up at me through moist eyes. It is happening. Are you ready?"

I nod. Another hard press of the baby's head causes me to suck in a breath.

Just try to relax and breathe, cara. *Just breathe.*

I begin taking deep cleansing breaths, which makes the growing pressure easier to handle. There is absolutely no pain, just the pressure of the baby readying himself to enter the world. When it increases tenfold, a rush of energy sweeps over me and I know it is time to push, which I do with all my might.

In the blink of an eye, Sebastian is holding our son. He cleans out little Antonio's nose and mouth. The moment our son takes his first breath and his loud cry echoes off the cave walls, an immediate change surges through the atmosphere. The feel of it is so powerful, we hold him between us and weep with joy.

* * *

Challissians exit houses and buildings, dropping to their knees, knowing immediately that the prophecy has been fulfilled and the golden child has come. Cries of joy ring throughout the city as citizens embrace one another, sharing their happiness.

* * *

On the surface around the north polar opening, the Urchins lying on the ground wounded but still alive, take a final breath, instantly disintegrating. Their ashes are blown away by a cleansing wind. Aaron and the rest of the warriors kneel, raising their faces toward the heavens, and with tears streaming down their cheeks, give thanks to *The One*. The long war has finally ended, and now will come the days of peace.

* * *

Mount St. Helens

In the palace room of the desolate, empty facility, the faint echo of Lord Derth's final cry rings against the stone walls as the last of his char-coaled remains fall from the satin-covered throne. One by one the walls crumble and the concrete ceiling falls. The whole facility caves in, leaving a large sinkhole a mile away from the volcano. Beneath the hole, not a trace of the building is left.

It is a fitting end. The being who had been honored and worshiped as a god by his creations, caring for no one, placing no value on life, and had even thought himself greater and more powerful than *The One*, dies completely alone.

Epilogue

We rebuild our home out in the countryside and every detail is the same. Our closest neighbors are the animals that protected me, their love for us spilling onto our son. At only two months old, thanks to Sebastian's daily communing with wildlife, Antonio knows and recognizes each and every animal. They are his friends and he is theirs. And Sebastian does indeed take him on a mammoth ride, laughing at my flabbergasted expression, grinning the entire time.

Motherhood is more joyful and fulfilling that I can possibly say. I am learning new things every day, and each time I hold Antonio and look into those piercing blue eyes, I see and feel the love of *The One*. I am indeed blessed.

* * *

Wrapped in my husband's arms, I hold our son close as we stand before President Simon in the magnificent white room in the sacred Building of Life, where he anoints Antonio for the second time and pronounces blessings upon him. His birth destroyed the enemy and saved the lives of many. Now he will inspire many and be a source of light, love, comfort, and strength for eternity, and we as his parents will forever be called blessed. Many other words are spoken, and they will remain in my heart always.

Walking us out, President Simon stops us at the door. He smiles, caressing Antonio's head. "I know you two have wondered if or when we will make ourselves known to the rest of the world."

"The question has crossed our mind more than once," Sebastian says.

The president nods. "There is a time for everything, which means there will definitely be a time for that as well. When that will be, only *The One* knows. But it will be soon."

"Thank you for telling us," Sebastian says earnestly. "We will keep this knowledge to ourselves."

"I know," the president says with a smile.

* * *

Putting Antonio down for the night, I join Sebastian out on the back lawn. We lay side by side, our fingers intertwined, and gaze up at our jointly-produced sky.

"It is not quite the wishing hour yet," he says, "but anytime is a good time to look at the stars."

Turning to him, I study his profile, so relaxed and at ease. "I agree."

He turns to me then, and in his eyes I see a thousand different emotions; I witness a thousand different memories, and I am a part of them all. In his eyes I see me, and the visions he shares with me through thought are like infinity. We have always been a part of each other. I see that now. Our story began long before I glimpsed him through my apartment window, and I knew him before this earthly existence. I feel as though he's been with me all my life.

Thinking on this, I softly gasp in awe. "It was you, wasn't it?" I pause and he smiles. "Throughout my life, I have felt this invisible comfort. It was you."

"I could never be away from you, Celine," he says softly. "I think our bond was formed long before our marks emerged."

He touches his mouth to mine, then lifts our hands, pressing our *Ki Talimai* together, igniting the warmth that neither of us can conduct with another soul. For our bond is true, it's real, and it's permanent, stronger than any and all other things, given and blessed by *The One*. And it always will be.

I am blissfully content.

And for the first time in my life, I feel absolute and complete peace.

About the Author

J. (Jewel) Adams stays crazy busy with her family and writing. She has written several books in different genres and is also a motivational speaker to both youth and adult audiences. She home schools her four kids that are still at home, and between that and conjuring up new ideas for her books, her brain is completely fried most of the time. She and her husband Sean are the parents of eight children, which means they are both losing hair, but hey, that's what Rogaine is for, right?

In her spare time (when she has any) she likes to curl up with a good book and a healthy stash of orange Tic Tacs. She and her family reside in Utah.

Jewel loves hearing from her fans, so if you would like to contact her to tell her how much you love her books or give her sympathy for the fried brain, or suggestions for the hair loss problem (for her husband, of course) contact her at **jewela40@gmail.com**

Also visit her website and blog at

jadamsnovels.com and **jewelsbestgems.blogspot.com**

Books by J. Adams/Jewel Adams

The Journey – YA Fantasy
Against the Odds – Contemporary Romance
Mercedes' Mountain – Contemporary Romance

E-books
The Wishing Hour – Romantic Sci-Fi Fantasy

Of Blessings and Dreams: The Legacy – LDS
Contemporary Romance

Tears of Heaven – LDS Contemporary Romance

Place In This World: The Sequel to The Journey – YA
Fantasy

The Journey – YA Fantasy

For Love of Angel – YA Romance

Elise's Heart – YA Romance

Children's E-book

Forbidden Portals: The Quicksilver Project

www.ingramcontent.com/pod-product-compliance
Lightning Source LLC
Chambersburg PA
CBHW072226190626
46809CB00017B/813